ZOMBIES
vs. NAZIS

Also by **Scott Kenemore**

The Zen of Zombie
ZEO
The Art of Zombie Warfare
The Code of the Zombie Pirate
Zombie, Ohio

ZOMBIES
vs. NAZIS

A Lost History of the Walking Dead

Scott Kenemore

Illustrations by Adam Wallenta

Skyhorse Publishing

Skyhorse Publishing books may be purchased in bulk at special discounts for sales promotion, corporate gifts, fund-raising, or educational purposes. Special editions can also be created to specifications. For details, contact the Special Sales Department, Skyhorse Publishing, 307 West 36th Street, 11th Floor, New York, NY 10018 or info@skyhorsepublishing.com.

Skyhorse® and Skyhorse Publishing® are registered trademarks of Skyhorse Publishing, Inc.®, a Delaware corporation.

www.skyhorsepublishing.com

10 9 8 7 6 5 4 3 2 1

Kenemore, Scott.
  Zombies vs. Nazis : a lost history of the walking dead / Scott Kenemore ; illustrations by Adam Wallenta.
    p. cm.
  ISBN 978-1-61608-250-5 (alk. paper)
  1. Zombies--Humor. 2. Nazis--Humor. I. Wallenta, Adam. II. Title.
  PN6231.Z65K47 2011
  818'.602--dc22
                        2011012302

Printed in China

For John Wheeler-Rappe (obviously)

ZOMBIES
vs. NAZIS

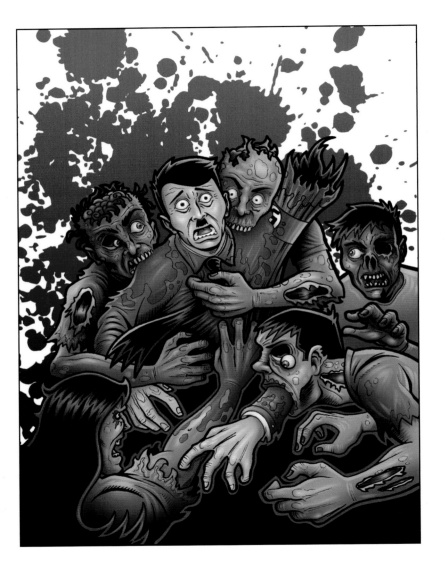

Preface

I'm something of an expert on zombies. I've written several books exploring man's relationship with the undead, and I continue to be amazed at how these creatures have shaped our world history. Then I read the letters reprinted in this book. Turns out that in the 1940s, the Nazis were hoping to create an army of zombies to fight for Nazi domination!

In these letters I learned that the Third Reich sent three Nazi operatives (Gunter Knecht, Oswaldt Gehrin, and Franz Baedecker) to Haiti to learn about Haitian Voodoo and, more expressly, to figure out how to zombify an entire army so that they could never die and would turn every one of their victims into yet another one of them.

Dumbasses.

Discovering these lost documents has only made it increasingly clear to me that humans are still too stupid to understand that **zombies never work for anybody**. They certainly don't want to be your soldiers. When you try to "employ" zombies—as couriers, as sugarcane millworkers, or as unholy knights of destruction in an army bent on conquering the world—**it will not end well for you.** Your plans will backfire, your project will fail, and you will get eaten by the very zombies you intended as your willing servants. End of story.

This fact is widely known, and yet every generation finds a way to tell themselves the lie that "this time, it will be different."

Um . . . no, it won't.

As this account should make amply clear, zombies aren't going to do your bidding. Zombies are just going to eat you. Whoever you are. And the more pride and hubris you have—and the more self-assured you are that your way of doing things is "the right way"—the faster the zombies are going to undo you utterly and turn you into mincemeat.

Thus, while many aspects of the Nazis' immersion into the world of VOODOO and the undead contained in this account are unusual and surprising, it should surprise no one that they made particularly appetizing subjects.

Read this account with serious trepidation, dear reader. And ask yourself a serious question: "Will humans ever learn?"

Now let us sit and drink and be merry,
And afterward, we will his body bury.

—Geoffrey Chaucer, "The Pardoner's Tale,"
The Canterbury Tales

U.S. Army Signal Intelligence Service
WASHINGTON 25, D.C.

UNCLASSIFIED

13 March 1940

MEMORANDUM FOR THE SECRETARY OF DEFENSE

Subject: Intercepted German communications regarding weaponization of the Haitian Voodoo "zombie"

The enclosed report contains translations of intercepted German communications sent between January 11 and July 6 of this year by three agents of the Nazi "Reichssicherheitshauptamt" (or RSHA), the Nazi information security service, who were stationed on the island republic of Haiti in the American Caribbean.

These agents were assigned to an espionage initiative exploring the possibility of weaponizing traditional Haitian religious and cultural rites for military applications. (Specifically, they desired to determine if the Haitian Voodoo "zombie" might be used to further German military objectives in the current European theater.)

Their regular reports to RSHA head Reinhard Heydrich were intercepted from U-boats transmitting off the Haitian coast and decrypted by the U.S. Army Signal Intelligence Service. (For your reference, each communication has been translated and numbered, but they are otherwise presented here unchanged.)

It is the recommendation of the undersigned that these communications be considered as informing any long-term strategy for American presence in Haiti and the Caribbean.

William F. Friedman
Bureau Chief
U.S. Army Signal Intelligence Service

COMMUNICATION 1

January 11, 1940
From: Gunter Knecht
To: Reinhard Heydrich

Obergruppenführer,

It is with considerable satisfaction that I report our successful arrival in Port-au-Prince, upon the island republic of Haiti. My colleagues, Inspectors Gehrin and Baedecker, have quickly established communications with their contacts in the biology department of the University of Haiti, and their position as visiting lepidopterists does not seem to be in any question. (The amount of field time a visiting researcher devotes to capturing and examining live specimens—in this case, the *Danaus plexippus*, or Monarch butterfly of Haiti—is typically very considerable. Thus, it should arouse little to no suspicion if they are observed in the Haitian countryside, and that they devote little time to being present at the actual university itself.)

Though I have yet to make contact with any of the local religious officials, my own position as a member of the clergy does not seem to be in any question. I am adjusting to the collar and cassock, and hope they may seem as natural as a second skin before much time has passed. (Though, in truth, I tremble at the thought of their effects during the tropical Haitian summer. The heat, I'm told, can be intolerable here. And yet, as the Führer reminds us, we all must sacrifice for the good of the Reich.)

As arranged, the university has supplied for us an acceptable dwelling on the outskirts of Port-au-Prince. It is a modern home of substantial proportions with a spacious study and an imposing mansard roof. The house is set apart from its neighbors and insulated from view by rows of trees that join with a thick forest at the back of the house. Inspector Gehrin has advocated forcefully for the additional construction of a research camp or outpost in the Haitian wilds. (He is concerned about the possibility of interruption or discovery.) As the leader of our group, I have filed this under advisement. Gehrin's suggestions are usually levelheaded and sensible, as is the man himself. I sense from him a great and earnest desire to be useful in furthering the purposes of the Reich.

Inspector Baedecker, on the contrary, continues to remain a source of concern. I do not hasten—though neither do I hesitate—to remind you that it was against my better wishes that he was selected for this assignment. My understanding is that his family is considered to curry favor with the party (though I can, of course, comfortably assert that no one could be in more favor with the Führer than you, my <u>Obergruppenführer</u>). And while Inspector Baedecker's natural bookishness, awkwardness, and propensity toward indolence may help him pass as an academic of some accomplishment, his lack of self-control (particularly when it comes to his consumption of sausage and beer) remains a constant source of worry. His girth makes him conspicuous in situations where remaining nondescript would seem preferable. His attitude, also, remains consistently negative in almost every endeavor.

Yet perhaps this is neither here nor there.

Per your directive, you can expect to receive regular field reports from Inspectors Gehrin and Baedecker—alongside my own, of course—regarding any salient elements we uncover. Despite my concerns regarding Baedecker's attitude, I believe we are excellently positioned to conduct a fruitful and productive study of the Haitian Voodoo faith, its supposed powers, and the possibility of adopting these powers for use on the battlefields of Europe (and, indeed, the world).

I will make it my foremost preoccupation to keep you updated on our impending successes.

Respectfully,
Gunter Knecht

COMMUNICATION 2

January 29, 1940
From: Gunter Knecht
To: <u>Reinhard Heydrich</u>

<u>Obergruppenführer,</u>

Warm greetings once again from the Republic of Haiti. Today, I am pleased to be able to report some early progress in our tasks.

Using the academic contacts of Inspectors Gehrin and Baedecker, I have made myself familiar with the religious studies department at the University of Haiti in Port-au-Prince. Through a minimum of inquiry, I subsequently secured introduction to one of the European religious representatives performing missionary work here in the city.

In the heart of Port-au-Prince, there is a cadre of several Irish priests—led, unfortunately, by a drunken oaf named Gill—charged with making large-scale conversions on behalf of the Holy See. In my initial meeting at their modest residence in the central district, they did not question my qualifications or mission as a Bavarian Jesuit. (This pleased me greatly, and attests to the skill of our research department in preparing an easily digestible dossier for this mission.) None of the Irishmen seemed inclined to express any open unpleasantness regarding current European tensions, either. I was welcomed warmly into their modest residence and given a tour of the city neighborhoods where their charitable and conversion work is performed.

Through Gill—whose tongue is regularly loosened, I gather, by the application of spirits from the Scottish Highlands—I learned that Catholics comprise the dominant European religious body in the country. However, there are also representatives of the Muhammadan and (alas) Semitic faiths. Then something intriguing! Taking me aside privately, Gill disclosed that—without the knowledge of his Roman overseers—he convenes a monthly meeting of officials from all three religious faiths. At this meeting, Christian, Muhammadan, and Jewish leaders gather as equals and speak frankly and casually about their efforts to reach out to the native population. In particular, they share schemes and strategies for turning Voodooists away from their native religion and toward more respectable faiths. (While there is, of course, some irony in Jewish mongrels converting Negro mongrels, I forced myself to nod along with Father Gill, as though it were a completely reasonable idea.) I am pleased to report that before our conversation concluded, Gill extended to me an invitation to join the next meeting of this secret council. As you will have deduced, it will be an excellent opportunity to learn more about the Voodoo religion, how its effects can be distilled and brought to our purposes, and the most expeditious way of reaching out to the local practitioners.

Efforts to ingratiate myself to this man Gill, however odious he may be, will obviously prove fruitful, and I shall continue to make them my focus in the coming days.

I am also pleased to report that Inspectors Gehrin and Baedecker have begun their own investigations in earnest, taking a somewhat more direct approach. (Updates from them should follow presently and provide you with greater detail.)

Respectfully,
Gunter Knecht

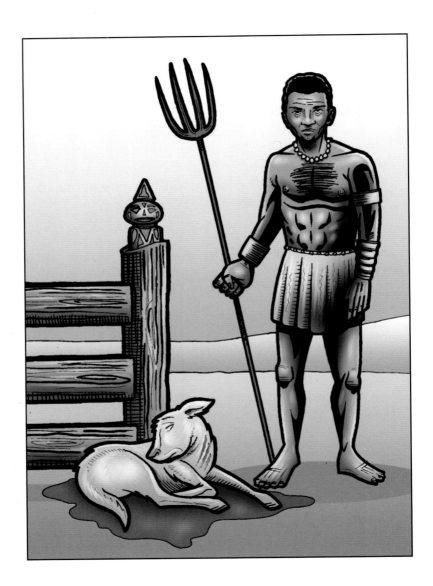

COMMUNICATION 3

February 1, 1940
From: Oswaldt Gehrin
To: Reinhard Heydrich

This is Inspector Oswaldt Gehrin of the Reichssicherheitshauptamt (RSHA), issuing first field report from Port-au-Prince and surrounding environs, detailing reconnaissance conducted by myself and Inspector Franz Baedecker for the purpose of securing zombie creation technologies.

My Obergruppenführer,

In any scientific endeavor, the collection of specimens from the field can be an ugly, inelegant, and even brutal process.

The most delicate samples are often gathered through the most indelicate of means. Pristine selections from the animal, natural, and mineral worlds are sometimes obtained only after local officials have been bribed, surrounding communities eliminated, and problematic interlopers summarily dispatched. To obtain sparkling diamonds, men must surely labor in some of the filthiest and most dangerous conditions known to man. To obtain another culture's darkest mysteries, one must associate with people and practices that are themselves filthy and dangerous. The efforts of the field are very different, my dear leader, from what you—as a man acquainted with the elegance of the laboratory—may expect of the scientist and his practices. Here in the field, we enter territory that, ineluctably, forces us to confront not only the more challenging sides of the scientific endeavor, but, indeed, of humanity itself. Therefore, it is my hope that you will forgive me if these field reports contain language and descriptions that stray from the clinical and delve into more vivid and visceral territory.

As Inspector Knecht will have already made clear, Inspector Baedecker and I arrived on the Republic of Haiti in the guise of lepidopterists from the University of Bonn. After introductions to our "counterparts" at the University of Haiti, we immediately set out to conduct field research under the guise of studying the migratory locations of the Monarch butterfly. In actuality, Inspector Baedecker and I have been surveying the Haitian countryside for the purpose of locating Voodoo activity (and using financial or other means to extricate information). Inspector Knecht has made it clear that he intends to essay a top–down approach to our assignment (connecting with religious leaders already in touch with the Voodoo community); thus, we are the bottom–up team, assigned to witness this phenomenon on the field level.

And I can report that we witnessed it almost immediately.

Inspector Baedecker and I began our investigations just outside of Port-au-Prince, in the series of communities tapering easterly into the Haitian countryside. While the locals we encounter display an air of contentedness and hospitality, it must—regrettably—be noted that the native Haitians fail to appreciate the state of depravity and defilement in which they exist. Various states of nudity abound— these subjects having prioritized comfort in the tropical climate above traditional notions of modesty and decorum. Women display their nude shoulders, feed their babies in public, and allow their legs to be seen well above the knee. Many of the men forgo shirts entirely. Inspector Baedecker and I were alone in maintaining a properly European modesty, despite the sometimes-stifling heat. (Inspector Baedecker simply required several rest periods—during which he prostrated himself on the ground and emitted loud gasping noises for several minutes, and thus found himself restored and able to continue.) This, as you will recall, is winter. Every fiber of my moral being rebels at the thought of what states of undress may pervade in this place during the summer months.

In our first useful encounter—occurring just three days ago—Inspector Baedecker and I espied a local farmer placing a carved figurine of the darkest African ebony upon a fencepost beside his sugarcane field. It was a clear day at noon, and we were striding through a more isolated region, carrying only our nets and specimen cases. Aside from ourselves and the lone farmer, there was nobody else in sight.

We moved closer, and saw that at the base of the farmer's fencepost was the body of a slaughtered goat. Its throat was cut, but no meat had been harvested from the body. We approached the half-naked farmer and began a conversation. After beseeching him, in the direst of terms, for a drink of water (which he provided us with surprising alacrity from a skin), Inspector Baedecker inquired about the significance of the figure and the goat. The farmer wasted no time in revealing that the two were the product of a Voodooist pact. Baedecker and I exchanged excited glances, and encouraged the farmer to expound.

A local priest—apparently named the Houngan—had provided the farmer with the ebony idol the previous Tuesday, during a ceremony in which the goat had been sacrificed to a Voodoo spirit called Kouzin Zaka. Under the terms of the ritual, in exchange for the goat, the farmer explained that Zaka would provide him a healthy crop and a successful harvest. If the farmer wished to ask Zaka for additional agricultural favors in the interim, he could do so by consulting the carved figurine.

Seeking to present ourselves merely as casually interested parties, we inquired after the Houngan and his abilities. The farmer replied that the Houngan was a local man, and that his office (called the Honfour) was regularly visited by the local Voodooists. The Houngan could ensure a good harvest, assist women with fertility issues, cure an infant's cough, and allow one to bring misfortunes of a supernatural nature upon enemies.

The creation of zombies is not listed among the Houngan's skills.

Though Inspector Baedecker seemed to indicate that the day's investigations had already yielded enough, I spoke up and pressed the farmer on the Houngan's ability to use Voodoo to turn people into zombies. At this point, the farmer became recalcitrant and uncooperative. It was only with the application of a significant quantity of local currency (printed notes known as gourdes) that the farmer seemed able to recall something on the subject.

He explained that the Houngan who serviced his community was a sort of general practitioner. For a procedure as complicated as the creation of a zombie, a *specialist* would be required. (I reproduce here the medical analogy because the farmer assured us that his Houngan would be able to make a referral—much like a medical referral—to a Voodoo specialist who *could* answer our questions about zombie animation.) The only additional facts the farmer seemed able to recall about the specialist were that his whereabouts are not generally advertised and that he is named Bocor or Baycor.

Happily, the farmer disclosed that a meeting with his Houngan could probably be arranged, and hinted that with the presentation of additional currency (both to himself and to the Houngan), a referral to the zombie-creating Bocor/Baycor would eventually be possible.

Inspector Baedecker and I have shared this update with Inspector Knecht, who seems pleased with our work. (At this rate, our path to the secrets of the zombie may be more direct and expeditious than we had expected!) An accounting of our expended currency (including gourde–Reichsmark conversion) is enclosed, as well as a formal request to the RSHA Office of Accounting for additional funds.

Yours respectfully,
Oswaldt Gehrin

COMMUNICATION 4

February 3, 1940
From: Gunter Knecht
To: Reinhard Heydrich

Obergruppenführer,

As you will have heard, Inspectors Gehrin and Baedecker have met with some success in their quest to reach the roots of Haitian Voodoo from the field level. I am pleased to report that I likewise continue to find success pursuing our objective through an insinuation into the country's ecclesiastical community.

Having received an invitation to join his ecumenical council, I joined Father Gill's gathering on the appointed day at the Catholic headquarters at Pétionville. (Gill continues to be a forthcoming and useful source of information, generally. With his help, I have quickly oriented myself to the neighborhoods of the city.) Before the meeting commenced, Gill explained to me that generations of Catholic presence in Haiti have resulted in many successful conversions. Converts abound, and many Catholic parishes flourish in the city and are growing throughout the countryside. However, when one scratches the surface, Gill explained, one finds a troubling phenomenon among many of these "converts." Namely, that many of them have merely incorporated *aspects* of Catholicism into their worship rituals while failing to shed the Voodoo tenets at the very core of their belief systems. To the eye of the visitor, these subjects outwardly appear to be true and earnest converts to the religion of Jesus. (Indeed, when Europeans are present, they are known to make a great show of forswearing the traditional polytheistic practices of their forefathers.) Yet in truth, Gill explained, they continue to worship Voodoo idols in secret, incorporating Catholic saints *alongside* their traditional deities. In the mind of the native practitioner, the "spirits" of the Catholic faith merely *augment* the spirits of Voodoo!

When asked if his Muhammadan and Semitic counterparts also encountered this problem, Father Gill responded in the negative. It seems that certain aspects of Catholicism—in particular, the practice of appealing to saints (the deceased) through prayers—particularly lend themselves to assimilation into Voodoo. After he had voiced this concern to me (and I had responded with commensurate shock and disbelief), Father Gill welcomed our guests from other faiths, and we began our gathering in earnest. Though tedious and overlong, the meeting was useful (inasmuch as the words of a Jew and Muhammadan can be said to be "useful").

Initially, the topics strayed to the mundane. The weather. The price of imported goods. News from Europe and the hope that current tensions might be resolved nonviolently. (While this "small talk", seemed pointless, I soon discerned some method to the madness of Father Gill. By allowing his disparate guests to find commonalities—the weather, the news, etc.—the irreconcilable aspects of their faiths seemed less daunting and problematic. It was a cunning tactic, and quite effective. After a few moments, brotherly love spread among all of them.)

After these preliminary remarks—and some excellent tea (Gill's, no doubt, "augmented" with whisky)—the unusual coterie *did* get around to a discussion of ecclesiastical work and the continuing influence of Voodoo in the country. All three faiths agreed that it was problematically difficult to "compete" with Voodoo in the mind of the native Haitians because Voodoo gave the (false) appearance of granting instantaneous results.

The Voodoo priest—my hosts explained—presents himself to the faithful as a "problem solver." When a Voodoo priest performs an incantation or spell, the faithful Voodooist then willingly credits the next positive occurrence (a much-needed rainstorm, the successful impregnation of a female, an enemy's unflattering weight gain) to the success of the Voodoo intercession. Of course, the faiths of the Middle East and Europe are very different. They have traditionally focused on salvation, the performance of good works, and providing answers to questions regarding the very nature of existence (as our own Dr. Heidegger now so excellently pursues). A Catholic in Dublin *may* pray to be healed of a disease—as may a Muhammadan in Mecca or a Jew in Moscow—but nothing in his religion tells him to count on the efficacy of this action. It is *possible* that God will intercede, but also possible that (in his infinite and mysterious wisdom) he will not. In sharp contrast, the Voodoo adherent has been conditioned to approach appeals to his religion in such a way that results are not merely possible but *expected.*

From each member of Father Gill's coterie, I heard that—bafflingly—the Voodoo adherent expects his prayers to "work" and "result in something," and to "actually make things happen that wouldn't just have happened anyway."

The serious frowns and grave expressions—shared by everyone in the room—attested to the deep and troubling problem these assumptions presented.

"But certainly," I essayed at one juncture, "the gesticulations and rites of the Voodoo shamans have only as great a chance of succeeding as those performed by leaders of our own faiths."

At this juncture my theological qualifications were called into question, and it was only through the recitation of my education and background in the Jesuitical tradition—however fictional—that I was adjudged fit to remain in the room for the remainder of the meeting.

Needless to say, I remained quiet for a long period. Nearer to the end of the gathering, I once again put forth a question cleverly designed to garner information.

"I still don't understand how the Haitian can find solace and guidance in any religion known all around the world for having such nefarious aspects," I began. "Just, as an example off the top of my head, the creation of zombies alone ought to be enough to alert any adherent to the unsound and depraved nature of—"

And here I was cut off, as the resident Muhammadan waved his arm to silence me—as if the room was suddenly filled with a noxious smoke, or bees.

"My Christian friend," he said after I had stopped speaking. "There are certain aspects of the Voodoo faith that do not bear to be dignified with explicit mention! In every religion of the world, there are practices and tenets that can seem . . . unusual or eccentric to outsiders. However, there are aspects of the Voodoo faith—and the one to which you allude is among them—that go beyond eccentricity, and venture into the realm of things forbidden by *all* faiths. In its chapter "The Prophets," the Holy Koran speaks explicitly against those who would appeal to gods from the earth to raise the dead. There could be no more explicit a warning from the Lord against the practice to which you allude."

"Indeed," the Jew chimed in. "And you will recall that in your own New Testament, Jesus is recorded as charging his twelve disciples—and them alone—with raising the dead. For all others, the act was forbidden. Some would say, then, that the most pernicious aspect of Voodoo is that men use it to intrude upon space that is the sole province of gods and prophets."

"That's the book of Matthew, chapter 10, verse 8," Gill chimed in, displaying—I thought—a very good memory for someone so dedicated to intoxicants. "And I believe the very same book also commands the casting out of devils. And that is an urging that all of us—not merely disciples of Jesus—can follow. The devils of Voodoo hurt Haitians by giving them false hopes and unreal expectations. All that we can do is shine the light of truth on them, and help them to see it."

Being summarily "corrected" by an Arab, a Jew, and a tippler was—as you might imagine—intensely grating. (It might have noticeably ruffled a less stalwart agent of the Reich. I was, however, outwardly unfazed.)

"Yet this unspeakable practice . . . ," I continued, "have any of you men seen signs of its presence firsthand?"

And here there was an uncomfortable exchange of glances that all but verified they would answer in the affirmative if they answered honestly.

"Some of us have seen . . . certain things," Gill allowed. "But we do not hasten to speak of them."

"*Where* have you seen these things?" I pressed.

Glances of discomfiture once again flew about the room.

"Tell me," said the Jew, "why do you wish to know such information?"

My superior training was all that sustained me against an outburst of rage and contempt.

"I simply wish to learn all that I can about local cultures during my limited time in this country," I replied coolly. "Who are we to believe that we can reach the local populace if we cannot first understand their world?"

There was some skepticism in the expressions that now met mine, but the Muhammadan spoke next:

"In that case—if your interest is indeed genuine and for the good of the Haitians' souls—I can allow that Bell's Hill, to the east of the city, is known as a place where these walking monstrosities have sometimes, been sighted. Though I hasten to add that my own experiences have been at a great distance and in the dead of night. I could not . . . swear that I have seen anything there."

Father Gill and the Jew exchanged a look that said perhaps the Muhammadan had divulged too much, yet neither went as far as to contradict what he had said.

Having secured a solid lead for further investigation, I quickly proposed a new topic (the evolving Haitian political landscape), and the members of Gill's ecumenical council were glad for the shift in the conversation. We continued with this pedestrian parlance until the meeting concluded, and zombies were never mentioned again.

With a little research, I have learned that Bell's Hill is hardly more than an hour's walk from the house where Inspectors Gehrin, Baedecker, and I are currently stationed! It is a lonely point—near an ancient burial ground with no headstones—generally avoided by the local populace. Roads run across it, however, and it is sometimes traversed by travelers—especially local merchants—seeking to save time.

I have, at the time of this writing, taken the liberty of scouting the hill myself during daylight hours, and have discerned no evidence of the zombies we so fervently seek. However, as ranking inspector, I have arranged for Gehrin and Baedecker to begin regular overnight surveillance of the hill. If the members of Gill's religious coterie are not lying, I expect results to emerge shortly.

Yours respectfully,
Gunter Knecht

COMMUNICATION 5

February 10, 1940
From: Franz Baedecker
To: <u>Reinhard Heydrich</u>

Inspector Franz Baedecker issuing first field report from Port-au-Prince, Haiti, and formally requesting a transfer to the battle lines, wherever the next available zone of combat should emerge.

My dear <u>Obergruppenführer</u>,

Surely, you can remember instances from your own life when you found yourself unsuited to a particular activity. Times when, despite a dedicated and earnest immersion in a new undertaking—archery, marathon running, a mastery of the Flemish tongue, etc.—you wisely concluded that for whatever reason, *you were not attuned for optimal achievement in this field.*

There was no loss of honor in your arrival at this decision. If anything, it showed evidence of an appropriately Germanic dedication to making one's strengths as powerful as possible (and neglecting the inefficiency incumbent on improving skills that could only ever range from poor to average).

Thus, it is in the interest of achieving maximum efficiency and effectiveness—and, indeed, a desire to make the greatest contribution possible to the Third Reich—that I wish to formally request a transfer from my current assignment to wherever exists the most urgent need for soldiers in our ever-expanding empire.

A consultation of my service records will reveal exemplary performance in marksmanship, as well as superior marks in foreign language and diplomacy. I can, based upon this, imagine any number of service scenarios in which I can be more useful to the Reich than in my current capacity. From frontline infantry to a diplomat's post in the court of a king, I assure you, it is impossible to find a place where I would not be of more suitable service to the Führer than here in Haiti.

The current responsibilities assigned to me by Inspector Knecht are, speaking frankly, a poor match for my set of skills. (Indeed, one might go so far as to suggest that Inspector Knecht shows poor judgment in assuming a man of my carriage and temperament could *ever* be suited to the work he now gives me.)

I believe a brief example will illustrate this to your satisfaction.

Just as Inspector Gehrin and myself had found our first conclusive lead for this project—a Haitian Voodoo priest going by the name of Bocor, who is reckoned able to create zombies—Inspector Knecht ordered us not to pursue that promising line of inquiry and instead assigned us to adopt a midnight vigil upon an empty hill. This I cannot abide.

Inspector Knecht claims to have it "on good authority" that this location is prime territory for encountering zombies. There are several problems with this. To wit:

It is not our assignment to "encounter zombies." (Doing so, on unfamiliar ground and in conditions of darkness, may be dangerously unwise and result in injury or death.) Rather, it is our assignment to discover how they are made, and to capture this information for use by the Third Reich. Inspector Knecht's "phenomenological" approach to gathering useful information makes no sense. Agents charged with improving our munitions program do not do so by wandering directly into the path of explosions. We have little to gain by wandering into the paths of zombies.

After observing *nothing of use* in this first week spent atop Bell's Hill, I believe that it is not the case that the hill is deemed an unsavory place because of the presence of zombies. Rather, it is doubtless the presence of the highwaymen and robbers—who have accosted Inspector Gehrin and me *no less than three times*—that gives Bell's Hill (correctly) its reputation as a place wisely avoided during the overnight hours. (Despite killing two of them with our Lugers—and scaring away several more—I have no feeling of accomplishment. We were not sent here to assassinate members of a substandard species but to take zombie technology from them. These nocturnal shooting sessions do not further our purposes.)

Whilst forced to abandon our own lead for Inspector Knecht's, we may be running the risk of forfeiting our chance for an introduction to the Bocor, who *can* create zombies. (Which, again, is the thing we were sent here to discover.)

Because of these and other unsupportable difficulties arising from his management style, I here suggest to you that I am not a suitable candidate for serving under Inspector Knecht. I formally request, forthwith, my transfer to a different post (including a zone of combat, in which my being placed in harm's way will *further the interests of the Third Reich in some discernible way*).

Respectfully,
Franz Baedecker

COMMUNICATION 6

February 11, 1940
From: Gunter Knecht
To: <u>Reinhard Heydrich</u>

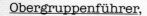

<u>Obergruppenführer</u>,

I trust that this finds you well.

To begin bluntly, I intuit that Inspector Baedecker is likely to have contacted you regarding his recent nocturnal efforts to locate a zombie on Bell's Hill. What, exactly, the content of this missive may have been is not known to me with any precision, but I will hazard a guess that he has taken pains to criticize my work and/or that of Inspector Gehrin.

While it is true that I have redirected the efforts of Inspectors Baedecker and Gehrin, I expect that any other details in his note are likely to be false and motivated by Inspector Baedecker's own remarkable underperformance during the past seven days.

Baedecker has exhibited weak-willed cowardice and incompetence at almost every opportunity. Most conspicuously, he has failed to disguise himself adequately, which is the first step in surveillance. Perhaps Inspector Baedecker's previous observational experience has been in urban areas (I no longer have his dossier to corroborate this hunch), but he has proven himself exceedingly unsuited to the Haitian forest. Disguising himself as what can only be described as a gigantic ovoid shrubbery (very much out of place with the indigenous fauna surrounding him), Inspector Baedecker has insisted on employing "disguises" that are more likely to draw attention to his position than away from it. Further, a distaste for the insects and small animals found in the Haitian undergrowth compels the inspector to position his giant egglike shrub away from any other undergrowth. In the best cases, this results in itinerant locals pausing only briefly to investigate the giant egg (or, fearing a trap of some sort, avoiding it entirely). In the worst cases, unsavory characters spot Baedecker from afar and instantly target him for robbery. (There is little, from his position in a nearby tree, that Inspector Gehrin can do to protect him, short of firing his weapon and hoping that the miscreants harassing our colleague choose to flee. In this way, Baedecker's horrible costume causes violence where none is necessary.)

Yet even with such egregious incompetence thrown into the works, the fundamental soundness of my plan to surveil Bell's Hill has nonetheless proven useful. Though he will likely have omitted this success from any report to you, the nightly watch has resulted in encounters with persons bearing obvious marks of association with Voodoo.

We have encountered old women wearing flags across their shoulders emblazoned with the symbols of Voodoo magic. We have seen herdsmen with animals doubtless destined for slaughter in the name of this or that Voodoo god. And we have spied elderly men walking with sticks carved to appear in the form of Voodoo totems, presumably for protection.

Despite the small risk to the personal safety of Inspector Baedecker (and, to a lesser extent, Inspector Gehrin), the week's watch on Bell's Hill has positively established the location as a thoroughfare of Voodooists. I stake my professional reputation on the likelihood that our vigil will produce increasingly useful results as our work there continues.

My Obergruppenführer, I do not know your level of familiarity with my Sicherheitsdienst (SD) and Reichssicherheitshauptamt (RSHA) training, and so I hope it will not be redundant when I reveal the following: During the course of my indoctrination into the SD, I was issued a kitten. Each day, as part of my training, I received a written instruction to spend no less than thirty minutes playing affectionately with my kitten, in addition to setting out its food and water. (I incorrectly assumed, as most

SD recruits do, that this exercise was designed to provide relief from the stresses of our daily regimen of exercise and study.) Then, on the thirty-first day, the instruction arrived that none of us had anticipated: I must kill the kitten with my bare hands. Obviously, this exercise is designed to test the dedication of SD recruits who might one day learn that a close associate, friend, *or another SD inspector*

has been proven to be an expendable traitor and thus requires immediate elimination.

Whatever your plans for Inspector Baedecker, let me disclose that I had no difficulty in obeying my order to kill the kitten when it came. Because it was a show of my unflinching loyalty to the Reich, I was more than a little pleased to do it.

Respectfully,
Gunter Knecht

COMMUNICATION 7

March 2, 1940
From: Gunter Knecht
To: Reinhard Heydrich

Obergruppenführer,

As important events are marked by the sound of trumpets blown on high, decrees from senior officials (such as yourself) or the Oberbürgermeister's tapping of the first keg at Oktoberfest, so let this humble missive trumpet and announce an important accomplishment by our task force of RSHA inspectors. For, lo! We have encountered the zombie!

My theatrical writing style may be forgiven (I hope). We are inspired by this success, which we earnestly believe will be of service to the Reich in the very near future. Whilst I was not personally present for this revelatory step forward, I can attest to the reports of Inspectors Gehrin and Baedecker (the latter of whom I may have been overhasty in condemning in my previous letter).

I carefully questioned both inspectors individually, and they were able to answer every query about their encounter consistently. What they divulged was this:

Whilst conducting—on my strict orders—their continued nocturnal vigil upon Bell's Hill, they chanced to observe two men of Haitian ancestry making their way up the hill. While one was disappointingly revealed *not* to be a zombie, the other man (or "man") with him *was*. While Inspector Baedecker's camouflage prevented him from interacting with the man and his zombie companion, Inspector Gehrin was able to extricate himself from his arboreal hiding place and strike up a conversation (and, moreover, learn valuable information about the zombie community outside of Port-au-Prince). I have directed him to write a full account of this interaction, which will be sent to you directly.

I must also note, however, a troubling development at the modest home that is our headquarters. It evinces the clear presence of anti-Catholic or anti-European sentiment on the part of the local residents.

Several days prior to this writing, I awoke one morning to find that a small man made of rope had been appended to the door of our abode. He had no facial features but wore a miniature version of the cassock in which I conduct my day-to-day errands.

At first, I guessed that this might be a tribute or a gift to a welcome visitor. Yet in a consultation with Father Gill, I learned that this was not a gift at all. Rather, it was a threat from the local populace. A threat to use magic against us. A threat that seemed to say, "Know your place, intruder. We are on to you."

Which was, of course, amusing to hear from Father Gill, who is himself not "on to" me at all, still believing that I am a traveling Jesuit.

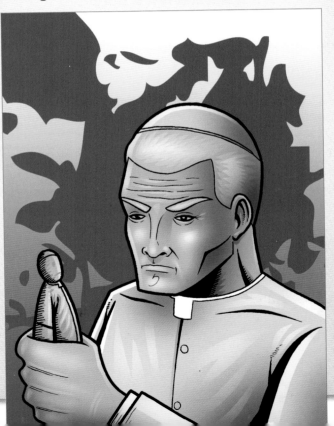

Yet for the first time, I saw something akin to frustration in Gill's eyes. When I asked why this concerned him—I was the target, after all, not him—he replied that agitations by the indigenous community tended to bespeak impending unpleasantness. This, of course, concerned me. I asked if I should be concerned for my safety. Then he said something confusing: "My dear Jesuit, it is the other way around." (I still do not entirely understand what he meant by this.)

Just this morning I found another doll awaiting me on our front porch.

I have resolved to keep a keen eye out for whoever may be leaving these unwelcome gifts, and to make an example of him or her with my Luger, if possible. There are a few locals I see regularly enough to suspect. Perhaps Baedecker or Gehrin has unintentionally offended someone at the university. Anything is possible among these heathens.

In conclusion, we are making progress, and Gehrin's description of the zombie encounter should follow.

Respectfully,
Gunter Knecht

COMMUNICATION 8

March 2, 1940
From: Oswaldt Gehrin
To: Reinhard Heydrich

My Obergruppenführer,

This letter contains details of our first encounter with an actual zombie. It verifies many hypotheses formulated at the outset of this mission, and disproves others. Most importantly (obviously), it verifies that zombies actually exist. Yet, as we saw that night on Bell's Hill, it also potentially amends our definition of what a zombie actually is.

Perhaps, my dear Obergruppenführer, you are familiar with the popular filmed entertainment *White Zombie*? It was released by an American movie studio in 1932 and features Mr. Béla Lugosi. I must confess that I, like many Germans, first formed my impression of zombies from viewing this film. (I enjoyed it greatly, seeing it more than a few times at the theater in Baden-Baden.) In *White Zombie*, the reanimated bodies lorded over by Mr. Lugosi's character were like robotic automatons. They stumbled forward slowly, their eyes unfocused, their senses numbed. Lugosi was able to command them, and they displayed perfect obedience to him. These zombies obeyed without question, like robots wearing the skins of dead men. (The application for such a perfectly obedient soldier in the cause of the Reich is, of course, easy to see.) These zombies would serve him, kill for him, or march themselves to certain doom at his bidding. *They were frightening because they could be commanded to kill, and they could not be reasoned with once given this command.*

I must report, however, that the actual zombie is even more troubling, alarming, and horrible to behold than those of Mr. Lugosi's film!

Just as the first sightings of mermaids by explorers in the New World were in fact only charitable descriptions of sea cows, so have descriptions of the zombie been rosily colored by the lens of the fabulist (and the lens of the Hollywood movie camera). The zombie that accosted Inspector Baedecker and myself was *very different* than the well-appointed butlers, obedient footmen, and sturdy millworkers portrayed in American films. In truth, Obergruppenführer, when described in total, the nature of the zombie we encountered may be shocking to you. Prepare yourself.

To set the scene: Inspector Baedecker and I had been waiting for some time under cover of camouflage when two shadowy figures approached our position on the hill. One was an older man of curious mien. His hair was long and braided into thick strands. He wore a dark apron around his waist, and his feet were entirely bare. His chest was bare also, save for the adornment of several rope necklaces that held strange ebon talismans that dangled together in a cluster. The heavy clack of these wooden ornaments told of his approach even before he came into view. (They seemed to weigh him down. I guessed they could not be worn for aesthetic pleasure but doubtless served some other purpose.) The old man gripped a metal chain, by which he led his partner, who stumbled like a drunkard and moaned audibly.

Yet as I stared intently at the man in chains, it became clear to me that something more was present. This "drunkard" was nothing other than a creation of the Voodoo shaman. It was a zombie.

Its eyes! My god, how can I describe the sight? There was no life in them. They rolled madly in their sockets in a way no living human's do—and yet they saw! (My skin crawled when the zombie's idiot stare chanced upon me. My blood chilled. My stomach knotted.) The zombie's rotting cloak was worm-eaten and reeked of a lengthy internment *beneath the soil*. Odors wafted upward, and from my elevated perch I smelled the horrible fumes of rot and decay that do not accompany the living. Yet most disgusting of all was its mouth. Between hideous low moans, the thing gnashed its teeth and slavered strands of drool that glistened in the light of the gibbous moon. It was a mouth that no longer spoke coherently yet longed to express some inexpressible inner longing that made the zombie stagger on.

It was with some courage that I descended from my spot and engaged the pair. (Inspector Baedecker was closer to our visitors, but instead of revealing himself, he took to shaking quite violently as they neared. As the man and his zombie paused to examine the large oscillating bush, I was able to approach them.)

I emerged from the foliage and identified myself as a visiting lepidopterist, in search of nocturnal Monarch butterflies. The Haitian man's first words, delivered in a thick accent, were an inquiry as to whether the vibrating bush nearby had anything to do with my research. As carefully and clearly as I could, I assured him that this was the case, and explained that the odd vibrations were related to my scientific experiments.

As we spoke, the zombie—whom he held at the end of a chain like a dog—slavered and salivated in my direction. Several times, the thing extended its arms as if to snatch my clothing (or scratch my throat), and each time had to be restrained by its handler.

Satisfied that the concealed Inspector Baedecker posed no immediate threat, the man took the time to caution me that I had selected a particularly dangerous location for my research. As if to drive home this point, the Haitian gentleman indicated the zombie he held on a chain.

Feigning ignorance, I thanked him for his concern on my behalf. Then, cautiously, I asked after the "man" on the chain, inquiring as to whether he might be insane, a criminal, or suffering from a tropical brain fever.

My ignorance seemed genuine, and it was with some amusement that our guest cautioned me that some things were better left unprobed. I quickly convinced him that, as a man of science, I took an objective and detached interest in the man who gibbered and snarled next to us. Our guest soon relented and imparted in hushed tones that the thing on the chain was indeed a zombie.

At this, the bush next to us vibrated again, and it took additional efforts on my part to convincingly attribute the

motions to a nocturnal butterfly mating ritual. When this was accomplished—and the vibrations had subsided somewhat—I asked our guest why it was that a zombie should be led through Bell's Hill in the middle of the night. He smiled—even as the zombie bucked and strained in his grasp—and gave a sly reply, saying that an important religious event was to take place nearby. When I asked about the chain—wondering if the zombie was being punished (or was uncharacteristically aggressive)—the shirtless Haitian laughed and responded that if I was a man of science (as I claimed), I was not a very good one. Zombies, he explained, were known for an innate aggressiveness and propensity toward cannibalism upon the living.

"I have heard of zombies sent as agents of murder," I explained to the man, "but you are saying that a zombie will attack humans in its . . . *default* state, without being directly ordered to do so?"

My visitor replied in the affirmative.

Yet when I pressed for more detail, his good-natured demeanor soured substantially, and he refused to speak further, hurrying away into the night (his wild-eyed, groaning zombie trailing after him).

Not wishing to abandon the constrained Inspector Baedecker, I elected to remain as our guests departed. Though no further surveillance was essayed that evening, several important and useful advances in our research have been made.

While it may be the case that the zombie we encountered was somehow atypical or anomalous in its aggressiveness, it is more likely that the aggressiveness of the zombie has gone underreported. This may be due to unreliable reporting, attempts at "cultural sensitivity," or the simple fact that those who have encountered these creatures in their typically aggressive state have not survived the encounter. (Indeed, even as I prepare these very words for the encryption machine, I shudder to recall the horrible look on that zombie's face. Its rolling, soulless eyes seemed to look into horrible distances beyond mortal imagining. Its teeth gnashed like a rabid animal's. Its hands were like talons, and they gestured violently as if to rip the air. It seemed capable of anything.)

Other questions are also raised by our encounter. Why did the zombie not attack its handler? Did the zombie understand verbal commands? (If so, to what degree?) Was it like a dog, able to comprehend a few basic words, or was it more like a human? Did it follow our conversation, or did it understand nothing of what we said? Did the metal collar and chain restrain the zombie, or were they merely used so that passersby would not be alarmed?

Clearly, we have more to learn, and our investigations here must continue.

It is my cautious hypothesis that while zombies still maintain the potential to be of great use to the Reich, in light of these events, we may have to reevaluate the specific role we expect them to play.

Yours respectfully,
Oswaldt Gehrin

COMMUNICATION 9

March 11, 1940
From: Gunter Knecht
To: <u>Reinhard Heydrich</u>

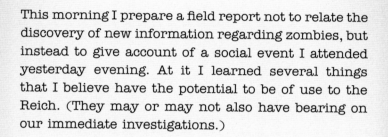

<u>Obergruppenführer</u>,

This morning I prepare a field report not to relate the discovery of new information regarding zombies, but instead to give account of a social event I attended yesterday evening. At it I learned several things that I believe have the potential to be of use to the Reich. (They may or may not also have bearing on our immediate investigations.)

Several days ago, during one of my increasingly regular visits with Father Gill, he informed me that he had been invited to a hospitality reception at the National Palace. The gathering of mostly European dignitaries and representatives would feature the president of Haiti, Sténio Vincent, himself. Gill insisted that this invitation should also be extended to me, and had seen that it was. Aware of the benefits of establishing proximity to those in power, I heartily accepted.

On the appointed evening (the tenth of March, last night), I joined Father Gill, and we traveled by

omnibus to the National Palace in the heart of Port-
au-Prince. The grounds were gloriously arrayed.
Regally festooned attendants welcomed us inside
(after some initial hesitation, as we were the only
guests arriving via public transportation), and
we found ourselves conducted to the center of the
magnificently appointed palace. As Gill had fore-
seen, the majority of the invited were international
dignitaries from places other than Haiti. (Truly, I
had not seen so many white faces since leaving the
airstrip in Jacmel!) And while there were several
representatives from the lands of our enemies—
France and England, certainly, were represented—
they were limited to boorish merchants and wealthy
gadabouts. As my dossier should confirm, I have
more than a little experience detecting the presence of undercover agents from foreign powers. I
saw none of them at this gathering. Every fiber of
my training told me that these French and British
bores were the genuine articles—penny-pinching
businessmen and idle socialites. (Thus, it was heart-
ening to imagine that even with so many countries
maintaining a presence in this little island republic,
only the Reich seems to have guessed the military
value of its Voodoo traditions!)

After a soiree consisting of hors d'oeuvres and liba-
tions (made with native rums) served in magnifi-
cent crystal goblets, the great gold-inlaid doors to

the inner sanctum opened, and President Vincent himself strode regally into the room. Though of dark skin and undoubtedly of African ancestry, the president bears the features of a European man (and also, sought to distance himself from his common countrymen with an affectedly displayed pince-nez and a sash vibrantly displaying the national colors). His tone, when he addressed us after our applause, was that of an educated man of breeding. (The assemblage regarded him nearly as if he were a man of Europe!)

Predictably (and despite my high hopes for a cursory presidential greeting followed quickly by some form of entertainment), the Haitian head of state made it clear that he had invited us here to draw attention to the Dominican Republic's massacre of Haitian laborers along its border. (It is the so-called Parsley Massacre of 1937, and was a feeble attempt by the Dominican Republic to expand its political power. Why the president of Haiti should be so aggrieved at the loss of a few thousand illiterate farmhands is quite beyond me, of course. Yet these are strange lands for the Aryan.) It should suffice to say that the diatribe was tedious and overlong in the extreme, and filled with details of the "atrocities" clearly designed to tug at the heartstrings of the audience. The president concluded his account of the incident by asking the European guests to beseech their home nations to exert international pressure on the Dominican Republic to pay reparations to the families of the slain.

When the speech finally concluded, we were invited to remain in the palace and finish what remained of the refreshments. I took this opportunity to approach the president directly and, through an artful ruse, to question him about the political entanglements of his island nation. (For as the zombie project continues, who knows to what extent the Reich's interest in this country may grow? It may not be enough to export Haitian zombie technology for the battlefield. We may also wish to prevent others from

acquiring it, through military means if necessary.) Thus, I used my Jesuitical uniform as an occasion to inquire which nations had supported development efforts in Haiti, and to which nations the Haitians, felt they could turn for support.

The issue of American involvement in the current European war—for who knows how genuine their declamations of neutrality may be—is an ongoing concern, certainly. However, after my conversation with President Vincent, I feel that the Reich has a staunch ally in him, whatever the Americans eventually do. In the international press, he is very much the puppet of Roosevelt (whose marines were in his country as recently as 1934). Yet I can tell that President Vincent is his own man, shrewd and cunning. (For example, he is aware of the extreme corruption within his own government, and also aware that his best course of action is to use the corruption to further his own interests.) From our not-inconsiderable conversation, I detected openness on Vincent's part to ally his nation with any friend seeming capable of providing protection and stability. *Any friend*. There is potential here for a really substantial return on our investment. And I daresay it would not take the entire Third Reich to protect the Haitian border from Dominicans armed with clubs and machetes. In return for this, we might enjoy unfettered access to Haiti's resources and the ability to openly study the weaponization of Voodoo as much as we like.

I will do my best to provide continued reports of anything salient occurring in Haiti's political arena. Meanwhile, our immediate task continues.

Respectfully,
Gunter Knecht

COMMUNICATION 10

March 19, 1940
From: Franz Baedecker
To: Reinhard Heydrich

My dear Obergruppenführer,

I hope that you are well.

Your curt response to my previous missive—and the obvious hastiness in which it was drawn—brings to mind visions of an officer dictating a response whilst under direct fire from the enemy, or a patient in severe stages of illness or injury (who struggles just to form coherent speech).

These, of course, are perfectly understandable reasons for delivering a response that—to the ear of one unfamiliar with the letter's circumstances—might be construed as curt, patronizing, and dismissive.

Thus, my dear Obergruppenführer, *I hope that you are well* . . . and have recovered fully from whatever danger or fit of madness seized you.

For the notion that your response was dictated from the comfortable leather chair in your oak-paneled office—the temperate afternoon breeze wafting gently through the window looking out on Prinz-Albrecht-Straße—is, frankly, unthinkable.

But let me—if only for the sake of our amusement—address this unthinkability. If not the duress of the battlefield or the deliriums of the sick ward, what other factors could have occasioned such a response?

Ignorance is one.

Ignorance, for example, of my father's place in the uppermost echelons of the Schutzstaffel (SS). Ignorance of the instances when *the Führer himself* has been a guest for dinner *in my family's home* might be another. Ignorance of the high places reserved for Baedecker men in the future Reich, yet another still.

But you, my dearest <u>Obergruppenführer</u>, are not an ignorant man.

Thus, I wish you a speedy recovery from any sickness and/or a safe return from the direct-fire battlefield location where you are currently stationed. I also repeat, in *the strongest possible terms*, my request to be transferred from the Haitian mainland to another assignment as quickly as possible.

If you see him, please send my regards to my father. (I have not corresponded with him in some time and hope, for your sake, it will not become necessary to do so.)

Respectfully,
Franz Baedecker

COMMUNICATION 11

April 3, 1940
From: Oswaldt Gehrin
To: Reinhard Heydrich

My Obergruppenführer,

I am pleased to report that our team has made additional contact with Haitian zombies. The salient details of this encounter run thusly:

After the successful encounter of March the second, subsequent overnight watches on Bell's Hill resulted in no less than three sightings in a four-week period. I write "sightings" because only in the final instance did I and Inspector Baedecker—who exudes a general reluctance to act hastily—interact with the zombies in question.

In the first encounter, we spied a team of armed men transporting what appeared to be a group of prisoners. The group was shackled in the manner of a work gang, and their chains rattled as they approached our hiding places. As they drew near, I amended my guess and wondered if it could be a group of insane being transported to an asylum. (Of course, my hope was that this guess would be wrong and we would see that they were in fact zombies!) The chained men gibbered and drooled like maniacs, and the guards urged them along with the butts of rifles—

correcting their loping trajectories when they wandered off their path. At the rear of the phalanx, we saw a stout woman who fit the descriptions of one steeped in Voodoo. She wore a headdress of beads and feathers, and clothes embroidered with wild patterns and bright colors. Around her neck was a rope from which a carved wooden figure dangled and danced upon her duggardly chest. Though the men around her prodded the chained figures, I saw that it was her own verbal urgings (sometimes augmented by a cane bearing the freshly decapitated head of a chicken) that truly urged the shambling parade forward. It was then that I understood for certain that these were not conscripts or schizophrenics, but fifteen or twenty *zombies* who were being transported past Bell's Hill (in, I noted, the same direction that our previous zombie had stumbled). I was intrigued, and strongly desired to interact with the group—as did Inspector Baedecker, or so I guessed from his excited vibrations—but we were outnumbered, both by zombies and armed guards. I reasoned that if the group should prove unfriendly, our Lugers might not be enough to protect us. Thus, we allowed the parade to pass unmolested. (Though there *was* a point when the Voodoo woman seemed to look directly at my position on the tree branch. Yet she did not acknowledge having seen me, and only smiled to herself . . .)

The second encounter occurred at the end of an evening's watch that had yielded no zombies (or passersby of any kind). I had removed myself from my arboreal post, Inspector Baedecker had extricated himself from his complicated foliage costume, and we were in the process of departing from Bell's Hill to return to our headquarters to sleep. Dawn was breaking around us as we walked, and this natural illumination allowed Inspector Baedecker to notice a group of five or six figures—who lumbered with the loosey-goosey gait of the zombie—silhouetted against the blue-gray dawn at the top of the hill. He alerted me to their presence with a more-than-adequate shriek. This allowed me to turn and follow his shaking finger as it reached, outstretched and trembling, toward the cavorting zombies. This group appeared at first to be unaccompanied, but upon closer inspection, we saw what has become a familiar sight: a human draped in the loud and unusual attire of the Voodoo practitioner bringing up the rear. Inspector Baedecker and I attempted to pursue this group, who soon lumbered out of sight; but by the time we reached the spot where they had been, all that remained were muddy footprints, a few scraps of torn clothing, and feathers from what must have been a very small bird. (Not a chicken.) Although it did not involve direct interaction with zombies, we felt this encounter was important because it established that the zombies *can* move about during daylight hours. The (presumably) mythological vampire, for example, is known to avoid sunlight on peril of destruction. Zombies are usually seen at night, but do they harbor similar nocturnal limitations? It appears that no, they do not. For as the morning sun fell on these undead subjects, they exhibited no discomfiture or alarm. Why, then, do we not see more zombies during the day? This is a question that remains to be solved. (I am confident, however, that this means a zombie army in service of the Reich would be able to attack, say, France, as effectively during daylight hours as it could after the sun has gone down.)

The final encounter was the most remarkable, and hints at deeper things, which we may be on the cusp of discovering.

It happened near midnight on the night before last. Inspector Baedecker and I were observing Bell's Hill from our customary positions when two figures came into view. The first was a hoary old man who waddled slowly and carefully. Around his neck were several of the totems of a Voodoo priest. He strode through the forest astern a single frail zombie who had sunken eyes and a great gaping mouth. On first spying them, I exchanged an excited glance with the bush that was Baedecker and readied my Luger. Here, finally, was a group we might overpower if we so wished. The older man was obviously unarmed, and the zombie looked as though it posed no threat that could not be contained by two hale Aryan men.

Unified in our purposes, Baedecker and I emerged from our covers at the same moment and confronted the figures, our weapons drawn. The waddling old shaman paused, and so did the zombie. (Near to the cadaverous thing, the horrible rot of the grave assailed my nostrils, and I wondered how the old man stood it.) Before anyone could speak, the old shaman began to remove something from his pocket. Mistaking this for a hostile gesture—for it was later revealed that he was merely reaching for a flask containing clarin, a native rum of crude distillation—Baedecker suddenly squeezed the trigger of his Luger, and the shaman fell to the ground, dead as a stone.

"Oh . . . ," declared Baedecker when the consequences of his action became clear to us. "Whoops."

Our human guest no longer with us, we turned our attention to the zombie. Its deep-set eyes were trained forward, unfocused, and it seemed not to regard us. It showed no aggression, and apparently failed even to notice that its handler had been executed.

"Well, it's not attacking us," I said, stating the obvious.

"What do we do now?" Baedecker asked, looking the zombie up and down.

"Can we take it with us?" I offered. "If we could safely transport the zombie back to our headquarters, I could take blood and tissue samples. We could then verify the claims of those who suggest the zombie is created through medical means, such as the introduction of a toxin to the living or the recently deceased. With the shaman dead,

Baedecker, we have no way of extracting any secrets from *him*."

"Yes, but . . . ," Baedecker began, and paused.

"But what?" I asked.

"But he hasn't got chains or a rope around his neck like some of the others did. How do we get him to follow us?"

"He looks light enough to carry," I said. Baedecker blanched, and I must confess I shared his revulsion at the notion of carrying the stinking, desiccated thing for any length of time.

Then, as if magically sensing our conundrum, the zombie began to shuffle forward. It moved slowly at first, as if merely stepping to correct its balance. But other small corrections followed. Soon they expanded into steps. The zombie then shuffled past us and followed the dirt trail into the forest.

"What do we do now?" Baedecker asked. "It's getting away."

"Well . . . very slowly, I suppose," I rejoined. "Let's follow it. Maybe it will show us something."

And so, Baedecker—still in the semblance of a small moving coppice—began to follow the zombie into the forest paths leading off from Bell's Hill. I went with him. It was strange work, like following a sleepwalking person. The zombie seemed largely unaware of our presence, and we strove not to "break the spell" that now made it ambulatory.

We walked deep into the forest. At every turn, the zombie displayed that it knew just where it wanted to go. It never hesitated when called to choose this or that trail. With supreme confidence, it directed us off the main trails and conducted us along smaller and smaller paths running deeper into the jungle. Soon we found that we traversed a path that might have been too small for a horse. Being a wide man in a costume, Baedecker began having some difficulty fitting past the underbrush.

After perhaps an hour of walking—with no discernable discoveries—we stopped behind the zombie and considered how to proceed.

"We have seen nothing," Baedecker pointed out. "I've changed my mind. Let us simply grab the zombie by force and take it back to our headquarters, as you originally suggested. It looks light enough."

"Wait a moment," I said. "Do you hear that?"

I cupped my ear. So did Baedecker. It seemed that on the edge of hearing, a deep and regular pounding echoed through the night. Who knew how long it had been there? Our own footsteps had drowned it out as we walked.

"It is a distant motor," Baedecker declaimed. "It is that, or the operation of machines in a factory."

"In the jungle . . . in the middle of the night?" I asked.

"Perhaps thunder, then, reverberating through the hills," Baedecker offered.

"But look," I said, pointing down at the zombie's feet.

The shambling cadaver, now a few yards ahead of us, was moving in time to the distant beat. For each resounding note, the zombie took another careful step.

"No . . . ," said Baedecker, doubting what we saw. "It is surely a coincidence of some kind."

"It is not," I countered. "He is no Kreutzberg or Wigman, but surely, this zombie dances to a beat!"

We regarded the zombie very closely. Its limbs moved in perfect time to the rhythm that resounded softly through the foliage around us. I soon saw from his face that Baedecker no longer doubted their connection.

"So what, then?" Baedecker said, after the zombie had danced forward a few more paces.

"Is he moving in the direction of the drums, drawn to them?" I wondered aloud. "Or do they command him to some other place, to some other task? I tell you, Baedecker, we will learn something valuable if we continue to follow him! If zombies are made into weapons for the purposes of the Reich, we will surely need to learn to control them. A drumbeat may be the very thing! Imagine giant radio speakers—perhaps mounted on airships or planes—beaming a beat to battalions of these creatures as they march across Belgium and France! What we learn tonight may be more valuable than what could be learned through the mere vivisection of a zombie."

"You are resolved, then, that we follow it farther?" Baedecker said, sounding disappointed.

I indicated in the affirmative.

Then the remarkable thing!

The zombie, who had lumbered no more than twenty yards down the jungle path—and was moving at the speed of an arthritic pensioner—was suddenly gone. When we looked up from our conference, the thing had disappeared completely.

"What?" I cried. "Where did it go? The zombie was there not a moment before!"

"It must have veered into the underbrush," declared Baedecker. My fellow inspector charged forward down the narrow trail to the point where we had last noticed our guide. There was nothing to see, but Baedecker continued to hunt madly for the zombie. I joined him, and we searched the woods as well as we could with our flashlights, yet our electric beams could never penetrate far into the dense Haitian undergrowth.

"There's no sign of him," my companion concluded.

"There is some mystery here, Baedecker," I said.

"Unless the thing broke into a sprint when our heads were turned," my companion rejoined.

"That seems unlikely," I said. "It looked as if it would shake apart if it attempted more than a jog."

"Should we continue down the path?" Baedecker asked.

I must here confess that despite the brave traditions from which I am wrought, I felt some trepidation at the thought of continuing farther into the dark jungle. I had only a general idea of where we were in relation to Bell's Hill and did not want to become lost. It would be difficult to gauge our position exactly until dawn.

Even as I paused to consider our next move, the beat in the distance continued to reverberate across the jungle.

"We shall continue down the path," I said to Baedecker. My confidence returned, and I reminded myself that a man of the Third Reich—the most advanced society in the world—could hardly have something to fear from a land of superstition.

"It is interesting to think," I observed to Baedecker as we strolled onward, "how it is that a society as primitive as the Haitian has stumbled upon so profound a secret as that of bodily possession and reanimation."

"Perhaps they are not as primitive as they look," Baedecker replied, having little use, apparently, for our Führer's wise opinions of the races.

"Nonsense," I countered. "Even a stopped clock is right twice a day, and even a fool sometimes hits upon an answer through sheer luck. Perhaps it is their proximity to the jungle itself that has given the Voodooists the luck of creating zombies first. This notion has always supported my hypothesis that it is a natural extract of some sort— derived from indigenous Haitian flora or fauna—that allows the Voodoo priests to create his zombies. Anyway, look at what the Haitians have done with it. By God! They have hit on the means of resurrecting the dead, and yet, have they used this power to assert their dominance in the region, or to extract a tribute from the Dominican Republic? No! They lack the intelligence and drive to use this power for any ambitious purpose."

"I do not know . . . ," replied Baedecker, his eyes downcast. "These Haitians may be wiser than you think. If we knew the secrets of zombies, perhaps we would not use them so freely either."

And with this absurdity, I raised my hand. (Initially, I did so to silence my companion's heretical speech, but in the space that ensued, we both discovered something.)

The noise was louder now. And there could be no doubt about what it was: the slow beating of many drums.

"What can this mean?" I asked. "Drums in the middle of the jungle . . . in the middle of the night?"

"These are like none I ever heard," Baedecker said. "No timpani or field drum has ever sounded thusly."

Suddenly, I spied movement in the jungle ahead of us and turned on my electric torch.

"Look!" I cried. Baedecker looked, and we both had time to see our slow-moving zombie friend pass just out of view, perhaps forty yards down the path.

"That's him," Baedecker said. "And he is clearly drawn to the drums."

I nervously extinguished my torch, and we continued after the zombie. It seemed now that the drumming grew louder—and more frequent?—with each step we took.

We fell silent. (Baedecker's insubordinately high opinion of the Haitian people needed further correction, certainly, but we both sensed that it was no longer appropriate to chat.)

The zombie came back into view. He was—for a zombie—moving quickly now (at close to the gait of a normal living person).

We began to see the flicker of large fires through the trees ahead of us. There was motion too. It seemed almost that the trees themselves bent and danced in the firelight.

"Bonfires?" whispered Baedecker.

The drums were very loud now. Multiple hands (or drummer's wands) clapped down with every beat, and the rhythms intensified. I estimated there were ten or fifteen drummers at least, all playing in perfect unison.

"And people," I added. "There are people just ahead of us."

I quickly understood that our project had once again changed. As the zombie danced ponderously toward the unseen drummers and conflagrations, I took Baedecker by the shoulder.

"It may not be safe to venture any farther," I told him. "But surely, we have found a site of importance to our research. I think the most prudent course of action would be to return to headquarters—carefully noting our route, of course—and to then return during daylight to inspect the site further for evidence and information."

Baedecker quickly indicated that my plan met with his approval.

"And yet," I added after a moment's reconsideration, "it might also be sensible to essay a glimpse of the proceedings, if we can do so safely."

Here, Baedecker dissented.

"No," I told him. "Having come this far, we must at least attempt an unobstructed view. Likely, some exciting ritual is taking place. Here, follow me into the underbrush."

We stepped off of the narrow trail and into the wet, sultry underbrush. I fell to my hands and knees—Baedecker did the same—and we began a careful crawl in the direction of the lights and percussive noises. The sound of the pounding increased with each step. (I mentally revised my previous estimates. There were thirty drummers at least—if not forty or fifty.) Our view was obstructed because of our semi-prone positions, but it seemed to me that I saw figures dancing in the shadows of the flames before us. These shadows, I decided, were men in masks, for their heads seemed unnaturally large and resembled those of animals more than men. As we drew even closer to the gathering, I smelled smoke, incense, and the scent of many people.

Edging closer still, I realized that the way forward was now directly obstructed by a boulder.

"Come, Baedecker," I said. "Secrets are ready to reveal themselves on the other side of this rock. Let us crawl around to the other side."

There was no answer.

"Baedecker?" I tried.

I looked behind myself and saw that my companion had suddenly disappeared.

I scanned the woods for him but detected no trace of my colleague. (I did not wish to risk using my electric torch so close to the gathering.)

Obviously, Baedecker's disappearance disconcerted me greatly, but I resolved that this journey should not be for naught. By hook or by crook, I would see what strangeness cavorted and drummed on the other side of the great boulder in my path! Edging my way around it, I began to detect bright flickering torchlight, the figures of dancing men, and the uniform motions of an array of drummers playing in unison like horrible, mindless automatons.

It was then that I heard footsteps behind me. I managed to make a half turn before the blow to my head rendered me unconscious.

I awoke at dawn, in surroundings that were momentarily unfamiliar. Next to me on the ground was Inspector Baedecker, heaped like a giant mound but, to my relief, still noticeably breathing. He had been stripped of his camouflage costume and wore only his trousers and nightshirt.

I stood and surveyed our arboreal surroundings. With great relief, I realized that we were back at the foot of Bell's Hill. Had we stumbled back under our own power? No. Several sets of muddy footprints leading away told the story of our having been carried back from the site of the ritual. (There were, I probably do not need to observe, a good many more sets of prints leading away from Baedecker than from myself.)

I walked over to Baedecker, intending to rouse him. Then I looked down into his face and beheld it. Ghastly mutilation!

Or . . . mutilation of a sort. For clearly, a lock of the inspector's hair had been crudely chopped away from the right side of his face, leaving his bluish white scalp exposed to the morning sun.

I roused him—at which he gave an awful start—and asked if he had any memories of the events of the previous evening. Like mine, his recollections grew fuzzy after we began crawling toward the drums and fires, and ended with complete unconsciousness. To my considerable disappointment, his memories proved no more useful than mine.

We returned to our headquarters and inspected ourselves for any other signs of injury, but found none. Other than painful bumps to the head (and Baedecker's unusual barbering), we have not been noticeably harmed.

We spent today recovering from this event. Tomorrow, we will attempt a daylight return to the site of the ritual. For whatever reason, the close encounter seems to have raised Inspector Baedecker's spirits. (He is normally given to not-inconsiderable bellyaching and complaining about our mission, living situation, and progress. However, an uncharacteristic calm has settled over him, and he remains nearly silent.)

We strongly believe that this encounter means that we are on the cusp of important steps forward in our research here. None of us doubt that we are close to something big!

Yours respectfully,
Oswaldt Gehrin

COMMUNICATION 12

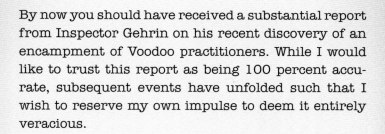

April 16, 1940
From: Gunter Knecht
To: <u>Reinhard Heydrich</u>

<u>Obergruppenführer</u>,

By now you should have received a substantial report from Inspector Gehrin on his recent discovery of an encampment of Voodoo practitioners. While I would like to trust this report as being 100 percent accurate, subsequent events have unfolded such that I wish to reserve my own impulse to deem it entirely veracious.

Inspectors Gehrin and Baedecker have now attempted—on multiple occasions—to retrace their steps and show me the places they discovered on their remarkable evening with the zombie. Each time, they have failed. The jungle paths are full of devilishly complex twists and turns and smaller trails that branch into others that are smaller still. However, none of these excuses the failure of our inspectors to recall the path they traversed with the zombie. All members of the RSHA are trained in tracking and should be experts at maintaining directional orientation in foreign territory. Gehrin and

Baedecker are no exceptions. If their tale is to be believed, then their own ineptitude risks forfeiting any value to be taken from it.

The inspectors *were* able to take me to the spot at the base of Bell's Hill, where they presume themselves to have been carried after being rendered unconscious. And indeed, the spot was covered with many sets of footprints. (Yet this is a well-traversed area, and to my expert eye, the prints looked as though they ranged from very recent to very ancient.)

Inspector Baedecker's hair is undeniably bobbed on one side. There can be no question of it. But as to how it happened, that is another matter. (Who can know if Inspector Baedecker is beyond a minor act of self-mutilation? He has been acting withdrawn in recent days, and this may be symptomatic of a man with something to hide.)

An instance creating additional concern for me occurred when Inspectors Gehrin and Baedecker attempted to introduce me to a farmer they had met in one of their very first expeditions into the Haitian countryside. They had claimed that this farmer confessed to using Voodoo to ensure the success of his harvest, and that he said that he could put the inspectors in touch with a practitioner who would acquaint them with a Voodoo priest who could create zombies. (They had criticized me for sending them to Bell's Hill instead of allowing them to follow this lead.)

I accompanied the inspectors to the farm in question. There did appear to be small, outlying indicators of Voodoo, such as a wooden idol on a fencepost, but little else. When we knocked on the door of the squalid farmhouse, there was no immediate answer. Though Inspector Gehrin asserted that we ought to wait for the farmer—conjecturing that he had gone to market or was otherwise indisposed—I drew my Luger and proceeded to kick down the door to his hovel.

On the other side, in a home of exceedingly modest appointment, we discovered the man identified by my colleagues as the farmer. He was quite dead, and had obviously been so for several weeks. His body was tied to a chair, and his head—apparently separated by several hacks from a cleaver or machete—rested beside it on the floor. From the mouth protruded several crumpled notes of Haitian currency.

Although they are trained professionals, I am having serious doubts about the ability of Gehrin and Baedecker to function as an independent unit. If they exhibit anything other than absolute competence and trustworthiness in the coming days, I shall be forced to start accompanying them on their nightly fieldwork.

Despite these recent concerns and setbacks, many strong leads remain for our investigation. I am confident that we are closer than ever to "cracking the zombie nut." Father Gill grows more and more receptive to my inquiries about Voodoo zombies. (Time and again, he shows that he knows more than he is initially willing to disclose). I believe it is only a matter of time before he reveals the next thing that will move our investigation forward.

Incidentally, word has reached us here of Germany's military engagement of Denmark. We shall raise a glass—Baedecker, no doubt, several—to toast this exciting event. May the Reich last one thousand years!

Respectfully,
Gunter Knecht

COMMUNICATION 13

April 17, 1940
From: Franz Baedecker
To: <u>Reinhard Heydrich</u>

My dearest <u>Obergruppenführer</u>,

When I was a child, my father insisted I attend the same boys'
camp each summer that he had himself attended. It was not far
from our manse in Gelsenkirchen—and many of my campmates
were boys who were already my friends—and yet each summer,
I resented being sent away with a violent intensity. I cried and
screamed. I pulled at the hem of my mother's dress as the house-
keeper yanked me away into the waiting Adler.

When my parents arrived on visiting day in midsummer, I always
begged to be taken home. (The sizable basket of sausages they
unfailingly brought me was little consolation for their imminent
departure.) I would cry until my eyes were red at the thought of
their returning to Gelsenkirchen without me.

And yet by summer's end—with all reliability—I would beg the
family chauffeur, when he came to collect me, not to take me
home. I would have forsworn anything—even the sausages brought
for the ride—for the opportunity to remain in my summer camp
with my friends for just a few hours more.

I tell this story to illustrate that extreme reversals of affinity—be they for a place or institution or region—are entirely within my character. The latest manifestation of this affinity is my strong desire to remain here in Haiti, under the command of Inspector Knecht.

I cannot begin to apologize for the language and tone of my previous letters. I will be the first to say it was as childish as my boyhood desire to return home from summer camp (and should be taken no more seriously than those tirades I delivered twenty years ago to my parents and their help). I will trust that you—like a wise father—have had the good sense to disregard them for what they were.

In recent days, an unexpected determination to remain in Haiti has suddenly washed over me. With a certainty I have never before known, I have the sense that it is in this land that I *belong*, and that there is something important I am here to do. (This, of course, can only be the work of the Reich.) When I try merely to recollect my previous reasons for wanting to leave the country, my head seems filled with a fog, and I am unable to cogitate.

Thus, in this missive I express my sincere hope that you have had the sense to ignore my previous communications for the childish rantings that they were, and I indicate that it is my sincere desire to further our purposes here in any way I possibly can.

Yours very respectfully,
Franz Baedecker

Postscript: Inspectors Gehrin and Knecht may have informed you of the loss of my costume that allows me to blend so seamlessly into the Haitian flora during our nocturnal investigations. Please know that I have begun construction of a replacement that I believe shall be far superior.

COMMUNICATION 14

April 21, 1940
From: Oswaldt Gehrin
To: Reinhard Heydrich

My Obergruppenführer,

As you will have been informed, after sharing the story of our recent adventure with Inspector Knecht, Inspector Baedecker and I have proven ourselves unable to locate the site of the Voodoo ceremony despite countless attempts. For this, I apologize. In selecting me for this mission, you doubtless considered my expertise in tracking and wilderness survival among the traits that made me an appropriate candidate (in addition to my considerable accomplishments in the laboratory). I have no excuses for this failure. According to my dossier, I ought to be able to retrace a few simple trails in the Haitian forest. My inability to do this—after *many* repeated attempts—boggles my mind (as I'm sure it does yours).

Yet it is not all failure here. I have good news to relate in today's report! No sooner did our inability to find the Voodooist's camp cast a pall over our investigations than an unexpected ray of light shone down from the heavens to bless our enterprises!

In the course of making my cursory monthly appearance at the biology department of the University of Haiti—and to apologize for the absence of Inspector Baedecker, who has been too distracted with the construction of his new "tree suit" to accompany me—I made the acquaintance of a young biology student named Jean Mayonette. He is a confident young man—articulate and obviously well read—though his speech is somewhat slurred by a striking harelip that all but splits the front of his face. After initiating a conversation about the migratory patterns of the Monarch, Mayonette began to speak to me confidentially.

"Professor," he said, "I have heard from trusted sources that you are often seen at night in the vicinity of a place called Bell's Hill. Tell me, is this the case?"

I was surprised by this question, but essayed to give an appropriate answer.

"I may have conducted *some* research there . . . in the course of our study of nocturnal pupae activity," I replied, seeking to maintain my cover.

"It is my guess that you may be interested in more than just butterflies," the young man replied. "And if

this is the case, then I might have something to show you . . . something that may interest you a great deal. May I inquire if you have plans to be near Bell's Hill this evening?"

Straddling the line of plausible deniability, I answered that yes, I would likely be along the road near Bell's Hill that evening, but only for the purpose of researching butterflies.

"Ahh," young Mayonette responded, "then perhaps I will have the luck to encounter you."

And he walked away, with no further explanation of himself.

Deciding to follow the strange lead—even if it promised a degree of danger—I holstered my Luger and made for Bell's Hill as soon as the sun had set. At half past ten, Mayonette made a conspicuous arrival, torch in hand. He strode confidently down the path on the hill's eastern side. I noticed right away that a shadowy, hunched figure walked behind him in the darkness. Of course, I hoped it might be a zombie, but—as has been the case before—it turned out merely to be an elderly person with a slow, loping gait.

"Professor," Mayonette called brightly through his harelip, "it is good to see you."

"Yes," I answered cautiously. "But I take it your presence here is not accidental."

"No," Mayonette confirmed, and he stepped aside to allow me to fully view the old crone beside him. "This is my grandmere, Marie. Many years ago, her husband—my grandfather—did some work for a local farmer. The farmer tricked my grandfather into going into debt. He refused to pay the farmer and made this fact publicly known. A few months later, my grandfather went to work and never came home again. Yet he has been seen countless times by those who once knew him. We fear that the farmer has gone to a Bocor under false pretenses and had my grandfather turned into a zombie."

"Yes," I said, "I believe I have heard of this Bocor gentleman before."

After furrowing his brow and glancing to the right and to the left, Mayonette continued: "I am telling you this because it is my sincere hope that—as a European man of science—you may have some insight into how my grandfather can be liberated from the legion of the zombie."

Ever an astute tactician, I instantly understood that this could be a way to familiarize myself with the process of zombification, whilst seeming to maintain a purely scientific interest.

"I may be able to assist you," I said to Mayonette, "but first you will have to tell me everything that you can about the creation of zombies."

He agreed, and proposed that we should adjourn to his grandmother's home, which he said was nearby. During the journey there, I made small talk with Mayonette (asking about his studies and so forth), but his grandmother remained completely silent. I began to wonder if she was capable of speech at all.

We arrived at a modest residence deep in the woods. Once inside, we seated ourselves around a circular table, and Mayonette lit a lantern and turned the wick low. When he spoke, it was in a whisper. There seemed nobody about (the house was fairly isolated from its neighbors), and it was by then the middle of the night, yet all three of us had the sense that our topic was something best discussed in hushed tones.

What Mayonette—and by turns his grandmother—disclosed to me flies in the face of much of what we understand ourselves to know about the Haitian zombie. It varies to such a degree that I am not certain if it can be credited at face value. Nonetheless, I believe it is still worth reproducing for your review.

Mayonette explained that contrary to what we have seen in *White Zombie* and similar entertainment, zombies are the bodies of the deceased that have been reanimated through supernatural means—specifically through rites performed by a shaman known as a Bocor. (Apparently, there is more than one of them.) Zombies are not,

Mayonette continued, created by the oral consumption of a zombie compound or poison. Neither do true zombies behave like persons under the influence of a hypnotic drug. (These are inventions of American filmmakers who reckoned that their audience would find a portrayal of true zombies too upsetting. Thus, they diluted the zombies until they were palatable for the silver screen's audience.) True zombies are the reanimated bodies of the dead, are innately aggressive and murderous, and are created through magical means.

I questioned Mayonette about the role of the Bocor. Does he control the zombie, I wondered. Mayonette responded that the Bocor's involvement is *absolutely vital* after the zombie begins to walk. The zombie will listen to the Bocor's verbal instructions (if it still has ears to do so), and can be further influenced by the Bocor's spells. A Bocor can, for a time, render a zombie as harmless as a kitten. Indeed, it is vital that a Bocor do so, for, left to its own device, a zombie reverts to a state of cannibalism and murder.

"In particular," Mayonette noted with some glee, "the zombie thirsts to eat your brain. If no Bocor commands it otherwise, this is the first thing a zombie will do."

"I have a question," I said. (In truth, I had several.) "If what you say is true, then of what use can European science be to your grandfather? You have just told me that zombies are reanimated corpses. Your grandfather is already dead."

"Precisely," said Mayonette. "It is for this reason that I require your assistance."

"To save him?" I stammered.

"No," retorted the boy, "to kill him once and for all!"

"His body should join his soul in rest," croaked the elderly grandmother. (I had been dubious of her ability to follow the conversation, but it seemed the words we spoke were not lost on her after all.) "He must not be the tool of dark deeds . . ."

"Yes," assented Mayonette. "That is it exactly. The Bocor and the farmer who killed my grandfather use his body to commit nefarious acts throughout the region. We must bring him to rest for the good of all."

"But . . . how does one kill something that is already dead?" I whispered into the near-darkness.

"There *are* ways, " croaked the grandmother.

Something in her demeanor turned deeply unsettling and eldritch, and I longed for a return to a two-way conversation between myself and the university student.

"Just as a zombie seeks to slake its thirst on a living, thinking brain, so are brains its own undoing," said Mayonette.

"A zombie can be killed—returned to the status of a normal corpse—by injuring or destroying its brain."

"Some say that removing the head from the neck also works," croaked the grandmother, nodding enthusiastically.

"Well then," I began, cautiously, "your predicament hardly seems impossible. I have brought a Luger from Germany capable of penetrating even the thickest of skulls. If you can show me where to find your grandfather, I can put an end to his status as a member of the walking dead with a simple pull of my trigger."

And, I thought to myself, *remove the grandfather's body to my headquarters for a thorough scientific study.*

"There is our conundrum," said Mayonette. "We know he roams the hills under the influence of the Bocor, but we cannot be seen looking for him personally. Those who interfere with practitioners of Voodoo have a way of disappearing, or worse. We do not wish to become zombies ourselves."

"I see," I told him, certainly understanding his position.

"But, you," Mayonette continued, "are perfectly situated to roam the hills outside Port-au-Prince whilst rousing no suspicion at all. We can tell you exactly where my grandfather has been seen. You could pretend to be looking for Monarchs. At the same time, you might make discoveries that no European scientist has made before. Who knows? Zombie discoveries might even be useful to you in some way."

I suppressed the smile rising to my lips.

"If I tell you the areas where my grandfather may be found, will you assist me in putting him back to the grave?" Mayonette continued.

Here, I began to play a dangerous game.

"You have correctly surmised," I told him, "that my professional interests extend beyond those of lepidoptery. And yes, I am intrigued by your idea. But I require something more."

"We have no money," the grandmother wheezed firmly. (It was a practiced declaration, no doubt honed upon generations of bill collectors.)

"You misunderstand me," I said. "As you have surmised, what I seek is knowledge. If I locate and 'put down' your grandfather, I will require you to introduce me to one of these Bocors who create the zombies in the first place."

Mayonette and his grandmother exchanged a long glance. Then the grandmother nodded.

"We are acquainted with someone who might be able to assist you," Mayonette said carefully.

We then laid out the specific terms of what Mayonette would provide in exchange for my being his contract killer.

"Then shall we consider it an agreement?" I asked, extending my hand.

The lad shook my hand forcefully, and it was done.

I departed from the grandmother's home, cautiously optimistic. Who knows how far a native Haitian—even one seeking to better himself through a traditional education—can be trusted to honor an agreement forged with his word? (A European gentleman he is not.) However, after several false starts, I believe that this task presents a line of inquiry that may yet lead to the answers we have been seeking.

Mr. Mayonette has drawn me mapped coordinates to where his grandfather has recently been sighted. As soon as Inspector Baedecker has completed his new disguise—which he seems very intent upon making as perfect as possible—we shall take to the field in pursuit. It is my sincere hope that we shall return with a suitable specimen.

Yours respectfully,
Oswaldt Gehrin

COMMUNICATION 15

April 23, 1940
From: Gunter Knecht
To: <u>Reinhard Heydrich</u>

<u>Obergruppenführer</u>,

I have received your letter and would like to begin by thanking you for taking the time to offer your thoughts and suggestions regarding the course of our mission so far. I would also like to extend my sincere gratitude to you for not yet recalling me to Berlin "to face the harshest possible consequences," as you put it in your communication. Indeed, I have faith that our project here can regain its focus and prove a successful one. I am well aware that every moment that passes is another in which zombie Nazis are *not* marching across Europe in a glorious orgy of death and destruction. Likewise, the notion that inferior peoples and races are currently required to be killed by actual living Nazi soldiers is as offensive to me as it is to you.

Trust me, <u>Obergruppenführer</u>, no one could be more upset by this unsupportable obscenity than I am.

As regards Inspector Baedecker, his radical shift in attitude has been unsettling, but despite my previous concerns, I now count him among the most stalwart and enthusiastic supporters of the Reich and its mission here. Perhaps you are unaware, but Baedecker—who as recently as this month liked to sleep until noon whenever his schedule allowed—now seems positively bursting with energy to perform our tasks. His industriousness knows no bounds! Between crafting a new jungle disguise— after his previous one was stolen—and undertaking what he has called "personal research" into the Haitian jungle, Inspector Baedecker also maintains a nightly security watch of our headquarters here on the outskirts of the city. Whether day or night, Baedecker can be found busying himself in some (apparently) useful activity.

Inspector Gehrin, too, continues to make useful forays into the mystery of the zombie. Recently, his findings are potentially revelatory—including that zombies can be made (or even, *must* be made) from subjects that are deceased. Inspector Gehrin also claims that it is *not* a Voodoo priest (or Bocor) who turns the zombie upon an enemy to murder him or her. Rather, the zombie is innately violent and murderous, and a Bocor intercedes only to *restrain* the murderousness or to focus it upon a particular target. Obviously, the idea of weaponizing an enemy's own dead to use against them is exhilarating, as is the notion that zombies would not require constant prompting to kill our enemies (but would do so always, *without* being prompted). I envision the Luftwaffe parachuting scores of zombies behind enemy lines, cannons launching zombies at enemies in fortified positions, and high-altitude bombers raining zombies down upon civilian populaces until capitulation is achieved!

My Obergruppenführer, it is all within our grasp!

I hope that I have convinced you that you have made the right decision in allowing our research to continue, with current team members still in place.

Yours very respectfully,
Gunter Knecht

COMMUNICATION 16

April 25, 1940
From: Oswaldt Gehrin
To: Reinhard Heydrich

My Obergruppenführer,

I have exciting—and troubling—findings to report in this update. Our investigation continues to take remarkable turns. First, I must relate that I have been successful in my quest to kill (or, perhaps, to "kill") the zombie grandfather of the university student Mayonette.

As you will recall, Mayonette had indicated the locations where his grandfather had recently been seen and had provided a description of the man. (It can be difficult to distinguish one zombie from another when they are in stages of advanced age or deterioration. Luckily for me, the zombie in question possessed a defining feature. He had no nose. It had been lost in childhood during an altercation with a wild dog. And while noselessness can arise from an older zombie's advanced decomposition, Mayonette assured me that I would know his grandfather when I saw him. And indeed I did.)

After just three nights' surveillance of a spot indicated by Mayonette (an abandoned outpost near a shuttered copper mine), I chanced to encounter the zombie I sought. He was just as had been described—the marks where canine teeth had taken his nose were unmistakable!—and he was alone.

I did not hesitate; I emerged from the underbrush with my Luger drawn. The zombie noticed me and lumbered forward aggressively. Ever the scientist, I did not kill it right away. Instead, I tested Mayonette's assertions about a zombie's points of vulnerability by leveling several shots at the creature's lower body. Great puffs of dust exploded as my bullets connected, and the zombie stumbled as the slugs disturbed its balance—but *it did not go down!* After a moment, it righted itself and walked as normally as it had before. It was only when I leveled my weapon at its head and fired that it seemed to be incapacitated (collapsing in a heap, exactly like a human who has been killed).

Under the conditions of our agreement, Mayonette would allow me to perform a full scientific postmortem on his grandfather's body. However, he first required me to bring the dead zombie to his grandmother's home so that—he said—they could verify that I had killed the correct one.

I placed the zombie in a thick burlap sack to insulate myself from its horrible fetor and ghastly appearance, and then hefted the sack over my shoulder. (Perhaps due to years of rot, it was surprisingly light.) Following my map, I returned to the hovel of Mayonette's grandmother. It was in the early morning hours when I arrived, but there was light from several lanterns flickering inside. Assuming Mayonette and his grandmother were still up and about, I knocked force-fully on the door.

"Hello," I called. "It is the professor! I have succeeded in my little task. Come and look."

Here, I hefted the burlap sack off of my shoulder, and it thudded to the ground before me.

No sooner had I done so than I heard the hasty unfas-tening of a crude metal latch. The door opened cautiously, and I was confronted by a hulking figure who was neither Mayonette nor his grandmother. The tall, wide man (who

was perhaps thirty years old), appeared to be a native Haitian. He had deep crevassed scars across his face and wore a headdress bedecked with feathers from a cock. A strong smell of incense escaped through the doorway past him and assailed me. It was not unpleasant. The man's expression, however, was. (I counted it a fifty-fifty balance of confusion and anger.)

"Hello," I said to him. "Is young Jean Mayonette—or perhaps his grandmother—at home? I have something of importance to deliver."

No sooner had the words escaped my mouth than two other gentlemen—of nearly identical age, scarring, and plumage—joined their compatriot at the door. They exchanged expressions of alarm and spoke to one another in a dialect with which I was wholly unfamiliar. (Note to RSHA Western Hemisphere Team: There may be more dialects, or even *languages*, among the Haitian Voodooists than our intelligence currently indicates.)

I attempted to explain myself, but the men became aggressive before I could finish my tale. One produced a pistol and pointed it in my direction. (Though I possessed a weapon of my own, I saw no reason to escalate the situation. I believed their anger was the result of some misunderstanding.) I raised my hands, palms outward, and began slowly backing away.

One of the large men leaned forward to investigate the burlap sack. When he had opened it enough to ascertain what was contained inside, he shouted in alarm. Then even more figures—I lost count, perhaps six or seven—emerged from the small house. All regarded the dead zombie in alarm. Their faces curled from confusion into rage, and several gestured in my direction. Sensing my options dwindling, I turned and ran into the nearest outcropping of underbrush, sprinting as fast as my legs would carry me. Some of the men followed, and at least one fired shots my way. Yet none of the bullets connected, and I evaded my pursuers by hiding in a tree until dawn.

This morning, I went directly to the university seeking to confront Mayonette. Not finding him on campus, I visited the registrar's office to inquire about his academic schedule in hopes of intercepting the lad on his way to class. Imagine my shock, Obergruppenführer, when it was revealed to me that *no student named Mayonette is enrolled at the university*. I also visited with the faculty members of the biology department. Individually and to a man, they claimed ignorance of a student named Mayonette (or any well-spoken student with a striking harelip).

As you can imagine, aspects of this encounter have been profoundly upsetting to me. We have, however, learned more about zombies (specifically, their temperament and vulnerability) than we knew before. Whilst we did not end the day with a specimen fit for dissection, we have been able to observe important behaviors in the field. Thus, I cannot say it has been an entirely bootless endeavor.

When I made my report of these events to Inspector Knecht, he suggested that we should return to Mayonette's house as a group and perform further reconnaissance. However, I pointed out that even with our entire squad present, we might still be outnumbered by hostile persons. Knecht eventually agreed with me, and I believe he is now considering alternative courses of action.

Yours respectfully,
Oswaldt Gehrin

COMMUNICATION 17

May 2, 1940
From: Gunter Knecht
To: Reinhard Heydrich

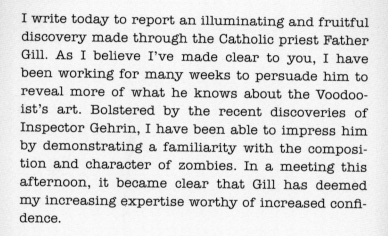

Obergruppenführer,

I write today to report an illuminating and fruitful discovery made through the Catholic priest Father Gill. As I believe I've made clear to you, I have been working for many weeks to persuade him to reveal more of what he knows about the Voodooist's art. Bolstered by the recent discoveries of Inspector Gehrin, I have been able to impress him by demonstrating a familiarity with the composition and character of zombies. In a meeting this afternoon, it became clear that Gill has deemed my increasing expertise worthy of increased confidence.

"My dear Jesuit," he began. (We were taking a leisurely stroll across the grounds of the Catholic headquarters.) "It seems clear that upon the subject of Voodoo, nothing can be kept from you. Because of this, I feel I shall lose nothing in disclosing to you additional facts that you would doubtless uncover on your own."

"Whatever you wish to tell me, please understand that I shall reveal it no to one," I lied.

"The purpose of my regular meetings with the Muslim and Jewish representatives in this country is not entirely motivated by the desire to foster a helpful exchange of theological information," he said. "I am also in a race against time."

"Whatever do you mean?" I asked, genuinely confused.

"I am an exception in the Catholic community here," Father Gill continued. "Through my fraternization with other religions—certainly—but also in my conviction that Voodoo's influence can be best mitigated through an openness and involvement with the communities that practice it. Most of the Catholics in this country are not in favor of my approach."

"What approach do they favor in its stead?" I asked innocently.

Here, Gill sighed and became deeply disconsolate.

"There are those who favor more extreme—and direct—measures," Gill said quietly. "Throughout its history, Voodoo has faced violent opposition.

Many in my sect would smile upon converting the Voodooists at the point of a bayonet. As any history book will tell you, Haiti has had European residents who frowned upon Voodoo since the 1700s. Every few decades—or, sometimes every few years—this disapproval has flared up into violence. Some years, it merely takes the form of isolated pogroms. Only a few people are actually killed. In other years, the entire countryside erupts in violence, and it is something more akin to religious war. I fear that another era of violence is brewing. We are due."

"And you believe it will come from the Catholic community?" I asked.

"I am sure of it," said Gill. "In truth, I fear that it is already too late to prevent it. My best efforts now may be spent simply trying to mitigate the level of violence, when it comes."

Father Gill then asked me if I had any pressing appointments for the rest of the afternoon. When I replied that I did not, he bade me to accompany him on a trek to the beach.

"It is one thing for me to tell you of these pogroms," he said as we walked. "However, it is another thing entirely for you to see the results for yourself."

We walked at a brisk pace, and I followed Gill for over an hour. We reached the coastline—empty, save for a few fishermen. Gill then led us down the coast, over beaches, hills, and past inlets, until we reached a cove where—noticeably—the fishermen began to thin out. As Gill steered us into the rocky crags, we became quite alone entirely.

"The locals are afraid to come here," Gill said, stating what I had already surmised. "There are plenty of fish in the waters nearby, but as long as they stay near *this* cove, they may have no fear of being caught."

He next conducted us down crude steps that had been hewn into the rock long ago. The way was treacherous. As an accomplished outdoorsman and well-trained RSHA operative, I was in little danger personally. However, it was remarkable that a drunken oaf like my companion managed not to take a spill on the narrow rock staircase.

Following Gill down the steep and precarious footings, I passed into the shade cast by the giant crags surrounding us. Though it was not late in the day, the shadows made it feel uncannily as though we had stepped through time into night. Soon I regretted not having brought my electric torch. I regretted it more when I saw that Gill was leading me toward a dark and gaping cave hidden at the back of the cove.

Just as I began to say something about the need for a light source, Gill produced two flashlights from the breast of his jacket and handed one to me.

"You'll need this," he said. "It may look dark now, but the place we are going is as black as pitch, even in the Haitian noon."

"The cave?" I asked, hoping, somehow, that there was a destination other than the forbidding darkness ahead to which Gill referred. (Truly, it was formidable. The mouth of the thing yawned ten feet high, if not more. It was easy to see that, a few steps in, the cave's pathway turned quickly to the right and prevented whatever lay beyond from ever seeing the light of day.)

"Indeed, that is our destination," said Gill, to my considerable dismay. "The locals call it Papa Legba's Mouth, referring to the Voodoo spirit known for his top hat and cadaverous face. In days of yore, the entrance would have been littered with boxes of tobacco and bottles of the finest cane spirits—offerings to Legba, and to the priests of the cave who served as his interpreters."

Now we crept into the mouth of the cave. There was no rum or tobacco to be seen, only the vacant, ominous darkness before us.

"Why have you taken me here?" I asked Gill as we turned on the electric torches and crept slowly inside the ebony tunnel.

"Because," Gill said, his voice now a whisper, "this is where the last pogrom started . . . and where it ended too."

"I see," I replied, although I did not fully understand what he meant.

Stalactites and stalagmites began several feet inside, and we had to maneuver carefully to avoid them. As we rounded the corner of the cave and passed into complete darkness, my beam hit upon a horrible face, and I gasped aloud. Moments later, I understood that it was only a face carved into the rock (a face with terrible, fanglike teeth and hollow, corpse eyes).

"Do not be frightened," said Gill. "For, indeed, it was the fright these images engendered that gave the place its power, I think. Look there."

Gill shone his flashlight far down the rocky tunnel in front of us.

"My god!" I exclaimed when my eyes followed his beam. "I would swear that to be alive if I did not know better. It's . . . it's *not* alive though, is it?"

What I beheld was a stalagmite the size of a human, carved in the shape of a hollow-cheeked man who grinned with glistening teeth of glass. A leather top hat sat rakishly askew on his head; onto his rock body had been sewn real garments. His stone fingers clutched an ancient glass that had once no doubt been regularly replenished with fresh splashes of rum.

"No, it is not alive," said Gill. "But it *was* alive in the hearts of the Voodoo adherents who worshipped and cavorted here amidst their strange, smoky dreams."

(Here, I thought Gill had waxed a bit too poetic, but considering our unarguably ominous circumstances, I gave him the benefit of the doubt.)

"Tell me what happened here," I said.

"The ground upon which we stand has been the site of horrible atrocities," Gill said matter-of-factly. "And I do not refer to the slitting of a goat's throat in any ritual. I refer to acts committed by Europeans who came here—waving the flags of 'civilization' and 'Christianity'—and murdered those they could not convert."

"What exactly did they do?" I asked.

"The last pogrom," Gill expounded, "was fomented in the camps of French missionaries, but the French were hardly the first Europeans to attempt to stop Voodoo through violence—nor, I fear, will history show them to be the last. When the French teamed with the former government to punish those who practiced Voodoo, the religion went underground— at least in and around Port-au-Prince. This cave was unknown to the French initially, and so—for a time—it served as a place where Voodoo continued to be practiced. I'm told that on some nights the worshippers in the cove outside numbered into the thousands. Yet it was only a select few of the initi- ated who were brought inside to commune with Papa Legba himself."

Here Gill motioned again to the hideously carved stalagmite. I found I did not like to look too closely at its empty eyes.

"When the French learned what was happening here, they sent soldiers with orders to kill," Gill continued. "On the night of an especially well-attended ritual, troops encircled the cove on the rock cliffs above, and a navy ship with twenty cannons blocked the retreat of anyone who might flee out to sea. They killed everyone, indiscriminately. When they were through, the waters in the cove below were tangled, with the flotsam of bodies, and red with human blood."

"And still, they were not successful in their mission," I stated. "Voodoo is known to flourish in the country this very day."

"No," Gill answered distantly, "they were not. Nor shall be anyone who attempts to use violence, rather than reason, to change the minds of others. If anything, the massacre at Papa Legba's Mouth *strengthened* the legions of the Voodoo faithful."

"Oh?" I inquired.

"Of course," said Gill. "For in the weeks and months that followed—by sheer coincidence, of course—a series of misfortunes befell the French soldiers who had undertaken the slaughter. The battalion that had fired down on the Voodooists began to exhibit symptoms of a strange poisoning that apparently led many to madness and suicide. The ship that had blockaded the mouth of the cove was lost in an unexpected squall and never seen again. And the French commander who had given the order to fire found himself bankrupt, lame, and begging on the Champs-Elysées in less than a year. As you will have guessed, these misfortunes were attributed to the vengeful wrath of Voodoo spirits."

With that, Gill led us back out of the cave. Though the rock walls of the cove blocked any direct sunlight, I was more than a little pleased to be standing in the open air again.

"What I fear," Gill said as we began the steep trek back up the cliffs, "is that history will only repeat itself, and that this time it will be a religion—our own—instead of a nation that is to blame for senseless murders that do nothing but perpetuate the zeal of the Voodoo faithful."

"Obviously, that would be a problem," I said, thinking as much of my mission as of Gill's predicament. (Engendering hatred between Voodooists and Catholics would not make things easier for a Bavarian Jesuit seeking Voodoo secrets.)

"Yes," Gill said. "And I am concerned it may happen sooner rather than later. Already, there have been isolated incidents of violence against Voodooists. I think this may stem not from a lack of hatred on the part of my fellow Catholics, but simply due to the fact that the Voodoo priests have made themselves harder to find. As you will have noted, Papa Legba's Mouth is not situated in a place that one discovers accidentally. From what I have heard, there are new places of worship located deep in the jungles."

Here, I could think only that this perhaps corroborated the tale of Inspectors Baedecker and Gehrin. Perhaps . . .

"I am glad that the centers of Voodoo have remained undiscovered, but I fear for the time when the next Papa Legba's Mouth is found," Gill continued between huffed breaths. (The steps were very steep.) "For each act of violence against the Voodoo community by outsiders, it becomes more difficult for representatives from *any* faith to make peaceful connections with the population in this country."

Here, Father Gill grew almost despondent over the chances of averting another Voodoo pogrom, but his musings did not contain any new information. When we reached the top of the cliffs, I soon excused myself and returned directly to our headquarters.

Father Gill's account was galvanizing to hear, if only because it makes it clear that we work within a finite time frame. If there were to be a large-scale anti-Voodoo uprising (and/or a corresponding backlash), it would severely hamper our efforts.

I have filed Gill's words under advisement, and insisted to Gehrin and Baedecker that their efforts be redoubled. I hope that this increased sense of urgency will result in a speedy and efficient resolution to our research here.

Respectfully,
Gunter Knecht

COMMUNICATION 18

May 6, 1940
From: Oswaldt Gehrin
To: Reinhard Heydrich

My Obergruppenführer,

Several days ago, Inspector Knecht shared with us the details of his trip inside Papa Legba's Mouth, a place of potentially important Voodoo significance. Inspector Baedecker and I have now visited this place ourselves. I can corroborate Inspector Knecht's impressions. Even without foreknowledge of the awful events occurring there, the otherworldly aspect of the cave (and the gruesome rock carvings inside) can hardly be overemphasized.

Despite Inspector Baedecker's protestations that his new jungle disguise was not yet finished, yesterday afternoon Inspector Knecht ordered the two of us to resume our forays into the Haitian wilderness. Ever obedient, we slipped into the jungles east of Bell's Hill and once again took up our search for Voodoo activity.

As we entered the networks of jungle paths, Inspector Baedecker donned his new disguise.

It was instantly clear to me that my colleague had not sought to duplicate his previous costume but had instead

reimagined it entirely. The disguise suit, as he now called it, seemed based upon a giant burlap sack from which sizable holes had been cut for head and limbs. The sack had been decorated with what I can only call pre-Colombian art. Many of the drawings were of recognizable shapes (pyramids, faces, animals), whilst others seemed composed of fantastical creatures (dogs with wings, lions with the heads of eagles, flying serpents). Then, on top of the various pictograms, Inspector Baedecker had festooned the garment with brightly colored flowers, feathers from birds, and the bones of small woodland animals. To top off his new outfit, Inspector Baedecker donned a cap decorated with a stuffed black-capped petrel (the entire bird).

It took me a moment to process the entirety of what I was seeing, but after a moment I regained enough presence of mind to gently ask Baedecker if his new costume was not slightly more conspicuous than his previous one had been.

"This suit improves upon several deficiencies in the older model," he replied. And this was all that Baedecker would say on the topic. Though he must have registered my many glances over his way—comporting, probably, a mix of confusion and disappointment—he could not be induced to converse further on the matter.

It was still dusk at the time of the moments I am describing, and I wondered if the suit might not have been designed with nightfall in mind. Yet as we crept deeper into the jungle and the sun sank from the sky entirely, Baedecker's suit seemed to take on an even greater appearance of strangeness. (Though to be entirely honest, something about his new costume seemed to fit and feel at home in a Haitian jungle. No one would mistake him for a large shrubbery, but neither did his festoonery feel entirely inappropriate.)

As we traversed the trails and jungle paths, I halted our progress at several points to listen for the sound of distant drumming. I was not sure if I heard anything. (There may have been deep noises on the edge of hearing, or they may have been in my imagination. It was very difficult to tell.)

I also paused whenever we reached a fork in the road—or a point where two paths intersected—to consult with Inspector Baedecker regarding which route we should choose. In past instances, this usually involved difficult (and, moreover, time-consuming) attempts to recall the details of the night when we had slowly followed the dancing zombie. (Indeed, we had failed utterly to retrace our steps for the benefit of Inspector Knecht in the days directly following the encounter.) However, on this evening, Inspector Baedecker seemed filled with an almost-preternatural surety regarding which way we should turn.

"Down this path," he might say, or "It was this way; I am certain of it," as we paused at the intersection of two virtually identical jungle trails.

At no point did I question or disagree with Baedecker's recollection of where we had walked before. (His determination to direct our progress into the undergrowth seemed trenchant and as though he did not desire it questioned.) However, after the third or fourth instance in which he claimed instantaneous knowledge of where we should go, I could not help but voice my amazement.

"My goodness, Baedecker," I said aloud. "Your sudden recollection of that zombie's path is remarkable. How is it that this knowledge has now come to you, my good man?"

In a stoic and serious voice, he replied, "I have dreamed of the way."

"Yes . . . ," I replied cautiously. "One can recall remarkable things whilst asleep. I am familiar with Dr. Freud's work on the nature of dreams. Have you read his published studies? Truly, more may be lurking beneath the surface of our minds than we know. I am also intrigued by the notion of his protégé, Dr. Jung, that dreams may be 'a window into the waking self.' Through this window, his theory goes, one can see things even more clearly than they can be recalled in a waking memory."

Baedecker only nodded in a noncommittal way (his animal bones and twigs jingling as he did so).

I did not question his divination of our pathway again.

We stalked deeper into the Haitian forests. I could not yet say if Baedecker's dreams were guiding us back to the site of the original Voodoo ritual, but certain elements of our environs did feel familiar to me. The sound of any drums, however, was still noticeably absent.

Then we rounded a bend in the path and suddenly encountered what could only be the giant boulder that had rested between us and the Voodoo ritual.

"My goodness, Baedecker," I whispered. "You have done it. This is the very place where we followed the zombie. We must make a map of the way and show Inspector Knecht. He will finally believe us now!"

My large colleague merely brushed past me and strode confidently into the clearing where the Voodooists had drummed and cavorted. I drew my Luger, switched on my electric torch, and followed after him.

The clearing was large (easily thirty or forty yards across) and, thankfully, bereft of life. However, a closer look quickly revealed signs of very recent habitation.

Enormous fire pits—some of which still smoldered—had been dug into the ground in several places. The trees that ringed the place had been decorated with curious totems and trinkets. Painted animal skulls, crudely stitched dolls (with eerily humanlike hair), and strange bright paintings adorned the bark of the trees and seemed to insulate the clearing from the jungle surrounding it. The ground had been trampled and bore the fresh prints of many bare feet. In some areas, the prints were clustered in shapes made by standing groups. Around the fire pits, the beam of my flashlight revealed patterns where whirling dancers had once leapt and gamboled by the fire's flickering glow.

In the center of the clearing was a low, flat rock that I quickly decided was an altar. It was circular and of the darkest volcanic rock. Upon it had been draped an intricately stitched cloth; and upon the cloth were the remains of candles, pewter dishes containing strong-smelling native rum, wooden rattles, small metal bells, ebon amulets on rope necklaces, and curious three-foot wands with chicken feathers attached at one end. There also appeared to be small photographs about the size of playing cards.

In the center of the altar was a recently slaughtered goat. Its blood had been allowed to flow freely, and the dark stain covered the contents of the altar and soaked into the cloth beneath.

"My goodness," I said to Baedecker. "What obscenity is this?"

As I ran my flashlight's beam over the cruor-coated collection, I perceived that the small photographic cards were not photographs at all but printed cards—similar to the baseball cards of the Americans—bearing the likeness and name of various Catholic saints.

"There can be no doubt," I whispered to my colleague. "This is the site of Voodoo rituals. We may learn much through surveillance of it."

Baedecker did not instantly respond. For a moment I feared that he had disappeared, and I searched the edges of the clearing frantically with my beam. Then the edge of the forest nearest me seemed to take a step forward, and I saw Baedecker emerge. (For all of my concern that his new costume would not conceal his presence, I had to grant that in *these* strange environs, it did so perfectly.)

"Yes," Baedecker finally responded. "This is a place of much learning, indeed."

"Right," I replied after a moment. "So listen, I'm going to scout around the perimeter to find an observation spot at the top of one of these trees. Then I think we should go back and report to Inspector Knecht. This place inspires in me a feeling of unease, even when uninhabited."

Baedecker only nodded absently and watched me walk away.

I stalked over to the clearing's edge and began surveying the trees for an appropriate perch. I needed a branch or crook that would provide an optimal view of the clearing whilst still concealing my presence. Ultimately, I opted for a giant juniper with a twisting, corkscrewed trunk. It stood a few rows back from the trees bordering the clearing and was in a position I felt would hide me well. The juniper was tall enough that I reckoned it would provide me a bird's-eye view of the Voodoo proceedings below. I was delighted.

Then I decided to ensure that the view from my new crow's nest was indeed optimal by doing a "test run" before we departed.

Would that I had not!

For you see, the darkness was so great that I knew climbing the juniper without my electric torch would be an impossibility. But then, with no illumination in the clearing itself, I would lose my geographical frame of reference once in the tree. (And Baedecker had, for some reason, forsworn his flashlight entirely. [Though I daresay that he seemed able to see in the dark with unusual acuity.]) Thus, before climbing the twisting juniper, I gathered fallen twigs and made a small fire in one of the pits. I stoked it until I was satisfied that it was bright enough to illuminate the altar in the center of the clearing and so would allow me to keep my bearings as I climbed the tree.

While Baedecker stood by the altar and watched, I quickly shimmied up the juniper and assumed a position near the top. My view of the clearing was perfect. From a spot where I would be quite unnoticed, I could look down and plainly see Baedecker standing by the altar. I was delighted. *But then I saw something more!*

As I gazed down at my colleague—thinking of all the future observations it would be possible to make from this position—I discerned a furtive movement in the darkness behind him. At first, I doubted my eyes and guessed it was the dancing of the flames that made it appear that I saw several sets of feet just behind where Baedecker stood. But then the sets of feet moved closer—in horrible, shambling lockstep—and I knew that they were no illusion. A few steps more, and I perceived that my colleague was moments from being overtaken by a group of horrible, rotting zombies.

These were no unwary Haitian citizens, killed and then reanimated to serve a Voodoo master. These zombies were rotting corpses that had lingered for months or years underneath the humid island soil *in graves!* As they stepped fully into the flickering firelight, I beheld that their skins were partially or entirely missing. Their lips had rotted away, leaving each with a maniacal skull sneer. Some were farther gone and had heads of more bone than flesh. Yet eerily, and inexplicably, their eyes seemed to be unaffected by the years of rot in the earth. Though their faces appeared like a surgeon's anatomy chart come to horrible life, these zombies had perfect, sentient eyes that glistened brightly in the firelight.

"Baedecker!" I called, all thoughts of concealment forgotten. "Zombies! Behind you!"

And before I could begin scrambling back down the juniper to assist my friend, I seemed to see Baedecker turn to regard the zombies. And though he must have been filled with as jolting a fear as one is likely ever to feel, his face remained placid and indicated no surprise at the presence of our undead guests. It was almost as if he were expecting them. (Truly, he is a stouthearted and brave servant of the Reich.)

I descended the juniper as quickly as I could, drew my Luger, and ran madly toward the fire pit that still flickered and spat.

But zounds! Baedecker and the zombies had *utterly disappeared*!

I conducted a swift search of the clearing but could discover no trace of them. The ground was so littered with foot-prints—now including my own—that it was impossible to tell in which direction they had moved. It was remarkable to think that in the short time it had taken me to descend from the tree, the zombies could have captured—or, I shuddered to think, *killed*—my colleague.

I continued to make circles, shining my flashlight wherever I could. Yet with each rotation of the Voodooist's clearing, I again found nothing. I became more and more frantic with each circuit. Eventually, a frustration overcame me, and I fired my Luger into the air, shouting, "Damn you, you zombie bastards! In the name of the Third Reich, return Inspector Baedecker to where he belongs this instant!"

For a moment, silence.

Then my call was answered by a deep and sonorous laughter that seemed to come from all directions at once. It is a sound that has haunted my quiet moments ever since.

In conclusion, Inspector Baedecker now appears to be lost to us. When it was clear that I would not find him in the clearing, I returned to our headquarters and shared the evening's developments with Inspector Knecht. Whether Inspector Baedecker can be assumed to be killed in action is not yet known.

I am not necessarily of the opinion that he is dead. Every prudent effort will be made to locate Baedecker, and our research continues in the meantime.

Yours respectfully,
Oswaldt Gehrin

Postscript: Please forgive this hasty appendage, <u>Obergruppen-führer</u>. As I left our residence to have this message delivered to you by our customary method, I found Inspector Baedecker's new bird hat resting on the doorstep of our house. (Baedecker himself—as a thorough search of the grounds by Knecht and myself revealed—was nowhere to be found.)

The hat appears undamaged, and I have taken it up to my room (where, with the help of several loud phonograph records now drowning out the sound of the laughter in my head, I hope to be able, this night, to get some much-needed sleep).

COMMUNICATION 19

May 7, 1940
From: Franz Baedecker
To: <u>Reinhard Heydrich</u>

My dear <u>Obergruppenführer</u>,

Having unburdened myself of the restrictions imposed by my colleagues, my research into Haitian zombie Voodoo continues. You will be notified of my progress in due time. In the interim, to expedite the success of our mission, please refrain from informing Inspectors Gehrin and Knecht of my continued service to the Reich.

Respectfully,
Franz Baedecker

COMMUNICATION 20

May 18, 1940
From: Gunter Knecht
To: <u>Reinhard Heydrich</u>

<u>Obergruppenführer</u>,

I am pleased to report that I have witnessed a remarkable ritual that I believe sheds further light on our understanding of the Voodoo zombie. The unfortunate loss of Inspector Baedecker notwithstanding, we continue to make substantive progress here in the country. (I received your instructions not to bother myself with further searches for Baedecker's whereabouts. You are right, of course. He is probably dead.)

My witnessing of the important ritual occurred thusly: Voicing my continued interest in his "cause" (e.g., preventing another anti-Voodoo uprising), I gradually inveigled my way into the further confidences of Father Gill. Insisting that additional knowledge of the subject would allow me to better assist him, I argued that I must be allowed to meet with a Bocor personally and, if possible, see the creation of a zombie firsthand. After much argument and hand wringing (on Gill's part, obviously), he admitted that such a thing *could* be arranged, and

an agreement between us was eventually struck. Yet even at high noon on the day appointed—as we walked from his residence to the secret location where this meeting would take place—Gill still, seemed to harbor reservations.

"My dear Jesuit," he asked with some hesitation, "as it may pertain to today's proceedings, may I inquire into your degree of . . . worldly experience upon joining the order?"

Somewhat puzzled, I repeated the dossier of the fictional life of the Jesuit I am supposed to be.

"I see . . . ," Gill said after I had concluded my lengthy autobiography. "I think I can say, then, that it is safe to assume that marriage to a woman was never in your past?"

Pretending to be shocked and astounded by his impertinence, I said, "Father Gill, I am shocked and astounded by your impertinence! Such a question! I have always lived my life in accordance to the wishes of the Lord and messages I received from the Holy Spirit."

"Understood . . . understood . . . ," said Gill, waving away my well-acted protestations. "And yet I hope you will not be offended if I divulge the fact that

I cannot claim the same honor. For you see, I was married briefly to a girl in County Cork many years ago. She was tragically lost in an accident, and it was then that I took up the cloth."

"My condolences," I offered cautiously.

"The point being," Gill said slowly, "I have found in my own life that certain things that I surrounded mentally with mystery, awe, fascination—including, in my case, the physical act of love with a woman— proved, upon consummation, to be less sensational than I had made them out to be."

"Are you saying that you are concerned that zombies will somehow fail to live up to my expectations?" I asked.

Gill tapped his forehead with his fingers and considered.

"I am concerned," Gill said, "because once the mystery is dispelled—and you have seen a zombie for the first time—you must then decide what to do with this information. Will it challenge your faith? Will you stay true to your commitments? Only time will tell. But if your presence in this country is maintained only by a fascination with the unworldly mystery of the zombie, I advise you to rethink this meeting. What you know of zombies will be forever changed a few minutes from now . . . unless you change your mind and walk away."

Before I could answer Gill, and promptly dismiss the asinine "concerns" he had raised, we were distracted by a pair of men walking toward us. Or rather, *I* was distracted.

The men, who were elderly and of wizened demeanor (one leaned awkwardly with each step on an ancient crutch), wore thin shawls over their shoulders to shade themselves from the heat of the sun. Yet I noted instantly that one of the shawls seemed to be made of *the original forest costume that once belonged to Inspector Baedecker*. Gill noticed my distraction.

"These men approaching us are connected to the practice of Voodoo," I said quietly to my companion. "Do not ask how it is that I know."

"Yes," Gill all but stammered. "My dear Jesuit, you continue to surprise me. Yes. Those men are not intimately known to me, but I have seen them in the company of the Bocor we are going to visit."

I merely nodded.

"Your knowledge is so formidable," Gill continued. "It is a wonder that you need me to teach you about zombies, and not the other way around."

Onward we stalked through the warm Haitian day, the humidity soaking the both of us. The sun was fierce, and I was much relieved when Gill diverted us from the main road onto a path that took us under cover of foliage.

As I stopped in the shade to mop my brow, Gill said, "Do you see that house hidden down in the vale?"

He pointed to a place where the terrain sloped and a grove of trees sprouted in thick succession from the forest floor. Built into the edge of this grove was an old stone house with an empty doorway and no door.

"I see it," I told him, noting the thick green smoke drifting up from its small chimney despite the heat of the summer day.

"When we enter," Gill said, "I think it is best that you let me handle the conversation. I know that you speak the language as well as I, but you will be perceived as an outsider here. I have taken some risks in bringing you along. Our hosts will be wary of strangers, and I would hate for a miscommunication or misstep to undo any of the trusts that I have worked so hard to build with this community."

Though I found his words patronizing, I agreed to be silent throughout the encounter.

I followed Gill as he stalked into the shallow valley and approached the doorless house. While from a distance, the only indicator that it might be inhabited was the rising plume of verdant smoke. As we walked closer to the house, additional signs of life revealed themselves. A powerful odor—not entirely unpleasant—of incense, fire, and cooked meat pervaded the place. One could also glimpse moving shapes within the dark shadows inside.

Five yards from the gaping doorway, a man stepped out to greet us. He was an imposing figure—tall, without a shirt on, and his waist wrapped in strange, colorful swaddles. The man regarded Gill only for a moment, seeming to recognize him; but he let his suspicious, iron stare linger upon me as I edged toward the tiny house.

"Grandmarnier, it is good to see you," said Gill.

I raised my eyebrows as if to say, *This man is named after the libation?*

Gill glanced back at me to say, "Indeed, he is." (Though this surprised me at the time, in retrospect, I should have known that a drunkard like Gill would naturally associate with people bearing a relationship to alcohol in one way or another.)

Without a word, Grandmarnier turned. We followed him inside the tiny house, which turned out to be quite crowded.

Six men—not counting Grandmarnier—were waiting for us. Five of them appeared to be native Haitians and bore none of the exotic Voodoo trappings I was expecting. Instead, they wore simple work clothes and muddy boots. Aside from hemp necklaces and the odd tattoo, there was nothing about them to indicate anything out of the ordinary. (I went as far as to wonder if they were participants in what was about to occur, or only hired workmen.) The final member of the sextet was attired like Grandmarnier—bare-chested and with many colorful fabrics wrapped around his waist. He also wore paint on his face, in a strange variety of red and white and green hues.

"This," Gill said to me as he indicated the painted man, "is a Bocor."

Gill did not give the man any other name.

In the fireplace, a fire was raging. Its smoke was green, and its flames licked up in a variety of strange colors. The odor it gave off was one part burning wood, while the other part was some unearthly smell I had never before known. Clearly, something more than logs had been added to the unusual blaze.

Chained next to the fireplace was a live goat. A large metal basin had been set next to it, and in the basin was a long, sharp knife. (Clearly, the poor beast was not long for the world. It seemed to know it too, and sat in grim resolve with its head hanging low.)

On the stone floor, a thin layer of cornmeal had been arranged in a series of intricate patterns like the walls of a labyrinth. On top of this labyrinth—reclining, with his hands over his heart—was a deceased man, still in his graveclothes.

"So that you are not alarmed, let me explain what will happen when the ceremony begins," whispered Gill. "The Bocor's first task is to summon a spirit—some would call it a force—into the room. This spirit will help us create the zombie. However, it is understood to be a bloodthirsty specter, and can turn murderous if its hunger is not sated. Thus, the goat will then be sacrificed, and its blood will be offered up to the spirit, which will keep us safe. It is traditional to eat the goat after the ritual, although you may find you have a less-than-hearty appetite by the time that we are done here."

I regarded the condemned animal doubtfully, already feeling my appetite drain.

"Once the dangerous spirit is sated, the Bocor will, direct it to reanimate the body of the dead man," Gill continued. "This will be accomplished through mystical words, the playing of associated drums and chimes, and the application of powerful balms and potions."

Gill indicated a leather pouch worn by the Bocor at his waist, which I assumed contained the magical mixtures.

"I see," I said quickly. "And can you tell me the exact ingredients involved in these mixtures? Are they of native origin? Must they be imported to Haiti? I would be very curious to know the extracts involved and their exact apportionment. And of course, the nature of their application to the corpse."

"Yes . . . perhaps later," Gill said, dismissing me. "If we are lucky, after the ceremony, the Bocor may be willing to share that information with you. As for their application, once the ceremony begins, there should be no question as to how the mixtures are applied."

Instantly, I regretted not having had the presence of mind to bring a camera, or at least some form of recording device. I resolved to take the most precise mental notes possible.

"Finally," Gill continued, "the zombie will rise from the dead. As this happens, the Bocor will take steps to ensure the zombie is contained. As the dangerous spirit vanishes, the dangerous zombie will emerge."

"And these containments?" I asked. "How are they effected?"

Gill again indicated that all would be revealed during the ceremony.

Moments later, Grandmarnier ushered the five workmen out of the small house. They departed obediently and seemed to disperse once they were outside.

"Be attentive," Gill said to me quietly. "It begins."

I followed Gill's example and sat down on the dirt floor. Grandmarnier—who seemed to be acting as an assistant to the Bocor—fetched a staff leaning against the wall and handed it to the old man. Grandmarnier then took up a drum and began to play a thunderous, unnecessarily loud (it seemed to me) cadence. The Bocor closed his eyes and began to speak in low tones in time to the cadence. As he spoke, he thrummed his staff against the ground, also in time to the beat.

As they went about their magical work, I let my eyes drift down to the motionless corpse before us. I must admit, there was an almost-electric excitement in the air. I looked hard for any movement or reaction in the cadaver, but there was none. I decided it must, of course, be too early in the proceedings.

Then a very singular thing happened.

A loud commotion could be heard taking place just outside the little house. From out of nowhere, I heard scuffling, raised voices, and muffled cries. Though alarmed, I hesitated to rise from my seated position at the ritual. (Not only was I about to learn invaluable information, but I feared that if I interrupted, or "broke the spell" of the magic, I might be censured from, or even forbidden to be present in, future ceremonies.) I remained silent despite the strange noises outside. (I did hazard a glance over at Gill, but his placid ruddy face betrayed no indication that he heard the fracas above the Bocor's rhythmic words.)

Moments later, I glimpsed distracting movement through the small house's doorway. I turned, and at that moment a group of men—perhaps ten of them—descended on us. They were all native Haitians whom I had never seen before. They were agitated and sweaty. They carried sharp-edged weapons, which appeared—alarmingly—to be stained with blood. Shouting aggressively, they pointed in our direction and let us know that we were to be the subjects of impending violence.

Gill saw them too and cried out. The Bocor stopped reciting his words, and Grandmarnier ceased to drum.

I leaped to my feet and attempted to draw my Luger, but was overtaken by the mob before I could do so. From out of the angry throng, a younger Haitian man emerged. He was better dressed than his compatriots, and horribly disfigured through a grievously uncorrected cleft palate. (Could this, I wondered, be the same cleft-palated man who had posed as a university student and interacted with Inspector Gehrin? I hardly had time to consider it!)

"This one!" he barked as two of the men held me down and wrestled my weapon from me (before, alas, I could fire a single shot). As I struggled in their collective grasp, the young man produced what appeared to be a velvet pouch from his pocket. Then he approached me and opened it, and I understood with sudden terror that it was a hood.

"Gill!" I cried out. "What do they mean to do to us?"

But I could say no more, as a ball of fabric was rudely shoved into my mouth. Moments later, the young man placed the hood over my head, and the world went dark.

I know not what befell Father Gill and the others, for I was next rudely conducted out of the small house, my arms forced behind my back and my hands tied. I was beaten about the lower body until I fell to my knees, and then struck hard on the side of the head by what I now believe was a repurposed cricket bat. The cessation of consciousness was instant.

Based on subsequent events, I can estimate with some accuracy that I was unconscious for approximately ten hours.

I awoke slowly. Even before I opened my eyes, I was aware that the velvet hood had been removed. I was, however, now tied around the waist in a standing position. Tied to what, I could not yet discern, though the ropes that bound me were clearly not tight, and I imagined I should easily be able to struggle free.

I lifted my head. I could smell the salt of the sea and hear waves lapping in the distance. Upon opening my eyes, I found only more darkness at first. Yet as I raised my head and adjusted my eyes, my circumstances became clearer.

I was in a subterranean place. The air was thick with moisture. The floor was stone or rock. I gazed about, and wished that I had not. It seemed that several silhouetted figures hovered ominously in the cave around me. They were the size of large men; some of them stood close enough for me to touch them with an outstretched hand. Yet as I watched them in terror, it . . . seemed they moved not at all, not even to breathe.

Am I, I wondered, in a place with dead men? Am I to become one myself?

But no, these were not dead men at all, or even men. For when I summoned the resolve to brush my hand against the nearest one I encountered only rock.

I instantly guessed where I was and confirmed it by reaching behind me to explore the thing to which I was attached by a rope at my waist. When I felt not only hard rock but also a buckskin jacket, a top hat, and a set of carved features (accurate down to each single tooth inside a laughing mouth), I knew that I was inside the cave known as Papa Legba's Mouth. More specifically, I stood tied to the statue of Legba, himself (in a position that, upon closer inspection, may well have indicated an intentional insult). The shadowy "figures" around me were nothing more than carved stalagmites.

My situation thus revealed, I took little time in extricating myself from the ropes that bound me. It was very, very dark, but because of my previous visit there with Father Gill, I believed it would not be difficult to find my way out.

As I prepared to feel my way along the rocky walls, my hand lit on the carving of Papa Legba to which I had been bound, and there I found my Luger, tied to his hand. (The bullets had not been removed, and I pocketed the firearm quickly.) After perhaps a quarter of an hour's work, I successfully navigated my way through the forest of rock to a point where I could see the open mouth of the cave. The moonlight shone off the calm waters of the inlet beyond, and I used their glare to navigate the rest of the way.

I emerged cautiously into the humid Haitian night, my weapon drawn and at the ready. Yet the scene was quite placid, and no aggressors attacked me. Though wary of another attack, I navigated my way up the cliffs and out of the cove, and returned to our residence without further incident. I did not sleep for the rest of the night, astounded and perplexed by the events that had befallen me.

Early the next morning, I lit out straightaway for the offices of Father Gill and his fellow priests. However, Gill was not at home, and his Papist colleagues could not account for his absence.

Now with a full understanding that further violence upon our person may be impending, Inspector Gehrin and I have armed ourselves against future attacks. We have opened the crate of MP 40 submachine guns and Model 24 ("stick") hand grenades that you so thoughtfully sent with us. Given the roominess of my cassock, it should prove easy for me to carry one of each with me at all times in a concealed fashion—in addition, of course, to my trusty Luger.

I have also taken the precaution of relocating our headquarters. I believe the house arranged for us by the university is known to those in the Voodoo community. (In a previous missive, I mentioned the totems that have appeared upon our doorstep.) Thus, I have secured a house of similar size—if of more modest appointment—in a more secluded area east of the city. This new house is, to the best of my knowledge, far removed from the site of any Voodoo-related encounters. It is insulated on one side by a nearly impenetrable forest, and its front door looks out on a large empty field where nothing ever happens.

Our work here will continue, but, my dear Ober-gruppenführer, it is clear that our approach must change. With the apparent abduction or murder of my most helpful contact (Father Gill), I believe it is now time to curtail my "diplomatic" approach to our operations in favor of a more direct line of inquiry.

Whilst we have already learned a great many things about the process of zombie creation—and the zombie itself—the task still remains for us to collect samples, attempt the vivisection of a "living" zombie subject, recreate a successful corpse-to-zombie transformation, and send the required ingredients back to Berlin for replication by the Reich.

In my opinion, we have learned all that we can from observing the practitioners of this religion from afar. We must now aggressively collect samples—using force whenever necessary—and compel those who hold Voodoo secrets to divulge them to us, whether or not they are inclined to do so. Have my assurances, <u>Obergruppenführer</u>, that we will show these godless heathens what happens when dedicated men of the Reich put their minds to something.

How do the Americans put it? "No more Mr. Nice Guy."

Respectfully,
Gunter Knecht

Postscript: News has reached us that the Reich is now pushing into France and Belgium. Huzzah! We shall, despite our strained conditions, endeavor to celebrate this accomplishment tonight with what passes for beer in this miserable country.

COMMUNICATION 21

May 30, 1940
From: Oswaldt Gehrin
To: <u>Reinhard Heydrich</u>

My <u>Obergruppenführer</u>,

As Inspector Knecht will have informed you, our research has taken a decidedly direct turn. After his unfortunate abduction—and, I understand, humiliation at the hands of a sodometically inclined statue—the inspector has directed that our activities moving forward shall consist only of two activities: 1) the collection of samples and 2) the interrogation of subjects regarding Voodoo techniques used to create zombies.

Under the newly enthusiastic direction of Inspector Knecht, we resumed a nocturnal surveillance of Bell's Hill. Per Knecht's new directive, we sought either a Voodoo practitioner (for interrogation) or a zombie (for vivisection). It did not take long for a suitable specimen to emerge.

After only a few days, I chanced to encounter a female Voodoo priest leading a single shambling zombie along the forest paths near the hill. It was the hour after midnight, and they were the only moving beings in sight. (I say "*I* chanced to encounter them" instead of "*we*" because Inspector Knecht had suddenly contracted a tropical fever and was convalescing in our new abode. Determined that a flu bug should not impair our work, I undertook that evening's surveillance alone.)

That this strange young woman was steeped in the Voodoo arts, there could be little doubt. She wore the heavy rope necklaces with dangling idols that I have come to realize are associated with the arts of the Bocor. On her brow was a headdress embroidered with colorful patterns of eldritch origin. In one hand she held a rope loosely tied around the neck of the zombie. In the other, she gripped a rattan cane with a cluster of cock feathers attached to one end. (It may be worth noting that our only previous sighting of a female Voodoo priest involved a giant ovoid woman who was mostly abhorrent to the eye. Whilst I thought this might be indicative of the typical physical manifestation of all female priests, the woman I now beheld was a striking example to the contrary. Her bosom was ample, but complemented by a modest waist and shapely hips. Her legs were long, and her long strides down the jungle path were a beautiful thing to behold. Though African of origin (and thus, as our Führer reminds us, inherently inferior to an Aryan woman), her beautiful features had a stunning effect on me, exhibiting a pleasing symmetry and appearance. I must confess that I felt a great engorgement of pleasure upon beholding this woman's visage and figure, having fraternized, you will recall, almost exclusively with men since the beginning of my time in this country.)

With my courage thus tumescent, I emerged from my hiding place and addressed the young woman and her zombie.

At first, she smiled pleasantly, and it seemed as though she would happily engage me in polite conversation. Then she espied the submachine gun swaying on its cord over my shoulder, and her face coiled into a horrible mask of anger. She emitted an audible hiss like that of a snake. (This caused my infatuation to dim somewhat, though not completely.)

Remembering my mission, I lifted the offending weapon and fired half of the clip into the brain of her zombie (a crusty old fellow who appeared to have been in the earth for many years). Its brittle head all but exploded, ripped apart by the gun's powerful blasts. The torso fell to the ground in front of us, still and unmoving. For all her serpentine bluster, the Voodoo priestess was quite disarmed, and she put her hand to her mouth.

I shoved my gun's hot barrel into the space between her breasts.

"You will now be coming with me, young lady," I said to her. "We have much to discuss. If you are forthcoming and honest, then you have nothing to fear."

She regarded me icily but did not protest. I moved behind her and nudged her forward with my gun. Taking back roads and discreet jungle paths to avoid being seen by any third party, I conducted her back toward the abode I share with Inspector Knecht. (Though I knew my compatriot was feeling under the weather, I hoped that he would feel well enough to help me interrogate this remarkable specimen.)

My guest remained silent as we trekked through the jungle. For a moment, I became concerned that she might be dumb. (An interrogation with a subject who could not communicate would obviously reveal nothing useful.) To test her tongue, I attempted a conversation.

"I mean you no harm," I said to her. "I am . . . a visiting scientist and student of Voodoo, only seeking to learn more about your great and historic culture."

Here, of course, I was forced to suppress a laugh.

"Am I correct," I continued, "in assuming that you are a practitioner of the Voodoo arts? A Bocor?"

At this juncture, the woman responded with a strange word I had never heard before (though it seemed she might be referring to a tropical fruit.)

"Come again?" I said.

"Mambo," she repeated. "When it is a man, it is a Bocor. When it is a woman, it is a Mambo."

"Ah, I see," I responded, thankful to see that she was capable of coherent speech.

"It's strange that the most basic distinctions of our religion are unknown to a 'visiting scientist,'" she declared icily. "Perhaps you are not a very good one."

"I—," I began.

"Am German," she finished my sentence in her own way. "I can hear it in your accent. Are you perhaps one of the visiting butterfly researchers who have been so clumsily bumbling about the area? We *do* wish you would all go away."

I did not reply.

"By your silence, I see that you are indeed one of them," she continued. "I also see by your conduct this evening that you are more than simply a student of tropical insects."

"It is enough for you to know that I am a faithful servant of my country!" I exclaimed, becoming annoyed by the precocious tone of my captive.

"As were the French before you," she said. "And the British. And all the others . . . back to the Spanish in the time of my great-great-great-grandmother. All of them were only faithful servants of their countries. All of them, eventually, decided to try to take things with the tip of a gun or a sword. Does it not concern you, my German friend, that all others have abandoned their projects here? Only a few outposts remain, and they are mostly staffed by harmless religious zealots whom we have learned to humor. What makes you think you are any different?"

I disliked the presumptive nature of the Mambo's question and the tone in which she delivered it. I remained silent for the rest of our journey.

Eventually, as the hands on my watch moved close to two in the morning, our circuitous route wound back to my headquarters. As far as I could tell, we had made the trip unobserved. No zombie footfalls pursued our own, and no ominous drums beat in the distance. Even so, to make our approach less conspicuous, I took us along the forest that abutted the house on one side—as opposed to across the wide field on the other—until we arrived at the back door.

We entered the dark, quiet house without event.

"Hallo!" I called to Inspector Knecht. "It is Gehrin! I have returned with a female Bocor—who is called a Mambo—so that we may interrogate her, per your instructions."

My calls were answered with only a low moan. The fever that had overtaken my colleague had been as sudden as it was severe. All afternoon he had been very sick. When he finally did emerge from the upstairs bedroom, I saw that Knecht was covered with sweat and could only support himself by leaning against the guardrail of the staircase.

As my sickly colleague slowly made his way down to the house's first floor, I busied myself tying the Mambo's body to a chair. She did not resist. As I secured her, she regarded my colleague with what can only be called an evil eye.

Knecht descended the old wooden staircase slowly and seemed to run out of energy upon reaching the final step. Instead of approaching us, he sat down on the staircase and rested his chin in his hands.

When the Mambo was tied quite tightly, Knecht motioned that I should approach him. I did so. He leaned in close and spoke to me in whispers.

"Gehrin, I am still very weak from this horrible fever," he rasped.

"I can see that," I said. "I am sorry to have roused you. I assure you that I am fully capable of conducting an effective interrogation on my own. Please, return to your bed if you are not well."

Knecht waved this idea away: "No, I insist on being present. I'm sure that you are capable . . . but even so, I wish to be here. "

"Very well," I said, turning my attention once more toward our comely captive.

No sooner did I swivel around to face her than the Mambo began to laugh. (It was not a pleasant laugh—no light expression of joy or delight—but the low, evil chuckle of a person contemplating revenge.)

She was not looking at Inspector Knecht or myself but, rather, out the window into the open field at the front of the house. Concerned that she had seen something, I rushed to the pane and peered outside. There was nothing beyond, however—only the empty sky, the short grass, and the low-hanging moon.

Frustrated, I slammed the window shut and closed the shutters. Then I stalked back to the laughing Mambo and turned my attentions to her directly.

"This is no time for levity, young lady," I said to her. "Let me be direct: My colleague and I are in the business of extracting information. We have been carefully trained in this art and are capable of making uncooperative subjects feel pain beyond their wildest imaginings. That said, if you are cooperative and forthcoming—which I hope you will be—there shall be no need for physical persuasion at all."

The young woman nodded seriously, yet a smile was still upon her lips. Although she clenched her teeth, an amused titter still escaped every few seconds.

"I see that you are not convinced," I said to her. "Have no fear. You soon will be."

I then took a chair from the kitchen and moved it in front of the Mambo. I sat facing her and took out my notebook and pen. I looked over at Knecht, who nodded in approval from his position at the foot of the stairs.

"We wish for you to tell us the means by which a lifeless corpse is transmuted into a zombie," I said to her. "As a female Bocor—a Mambo, that is—you are in possession of this information. You see, there is much that we already know about you."

Here she stopped her tittering and raised an inquisitive eyebrow.

"I see that I have your attention," I told her. "Yes, we are aware of much of the ceremony. The goat that must be sacrificed . . . the drumming . . . the designs drawn upon the floor and over the corpse in cornmeal."

As I finished this litany, the Mambo cast her eyes around the room as if waiting for the punch line of a joke. When it became clear that I had finished speaking, she once again broke loose with peals of dark laughter that seemed to spew forth from an evil subterranean cave within her.

"Yes!" she cackled. "It is clear to me—someone *has* made you aware of something, indeed. Haha!"

I did not have to look over to Knecht to know that he wished me to correct the situation. I stood and gave the jocular witch several hard blows across the face with the back of my hand. The Mambo presently fell silent. Though I had bloodied her nose and lips, she still managed to smile. I sat back down across from her.

"I can assure you that that was nothing, young lady," I said sternly. "If you will not become immediately cooperative, we shall begin the interrogation in earnest. My colleague seated on the stairs is not as kind as I. His predilections usually call for me to begin by removing a subject's finger-nails and teeth, and then to move on to more *serious* methods. It would be a pity if you forced me to disfigure a face as comely as yours, but you must understand that I would not hesitate to do it."

For a moment, the young lady only stared at me—still smiling, always smiling.

"Yes," she said with a confidence that seemed out of place. "I think that teaching you to raise the dead—here and now—is *exactly* what needs to happen."

"Good," I said cautiously. (Probably my tone reflected my surprise. I had not expected her capitulation to come so freely. Given the woman's fiery spirit, I was betting that the extrication of at least a few fingernails would come before any useful progress.)

"But you must untie my hands," the Mambo said. "There are certain . . . motions involved . . . that I cannot describe with only words."

"Very well," I told her, "but have no confusion. Any attempt on your part to escape will be met with brutal—or fatal—consequences. My colleague may be under the weather, but he can still shoot a gun. And the surrounding hills are rife with Bocors and Mambos. It would be a very small matter for us to kill you and obtain another."

The Mambo smiled icily as I loosened the ropes that bound her upper body, and she worked her arms free.

"Now," I said, taking up my pen and notebook, "how does one create a zombie?"

"There are many totems and trappings in our ceremonies," said the Mambo. "But these are merely decorations. Formality. The *real* power of the Bocor and the Mambo is in one thing alone."

"Yes?" I said, my fountain pen dripping on the page in anticipation. "And what is it?"

"A chant," said the Mambo. "The power is found in an ancient chant that has been passed down to a select few since the oldest days. It is older than Muhammad or Jesus or Moses. It is older than the first men who sailed in barks from sea to sea. It is as old as the Old Ones themselves, who are older than men."

"And how does it go, this chant?" I asked, hoping that my years in the conservatory would allow me to accurately record any musical subtleties to the incantation.

"I shall sing it . . . but then *you* must sing it with me," the Mambo said. "Two voices are required. It is one chant upon another chant. Therein may be found the power. Listen to what I sing now, until you know it well enough that you can reproduce it perfectly."

She then began an almost indescribably guttural and blunt-tongued cant. The words she spoke—if, indeed, words are what they were—seemed almost entirely devoid of verbs. There were animalistic clickings, spittle-filled stops, and trills of the tongue that were closer to the language of insects than men. As her mouth emitted these remarkable noises, the Mambo lifted her hands over her head and snapped her fingers to punctuate certain words (again, if words they even were). Her eyes rolled back in their sockets, and she seemed to enter a trancelike state.

At first I attempted to record the sounds with my pen, but it was quickly clear to me that I lacked the holographic lexicon for such an undertaking. (Looking back at my notes now, I see that I got as far as "XXthoxx Nthuxxx. XXthoxx Xthulu Xthulu Fghthxxxn. Xthulu Xthulu Fghthxxxn" before giving up.) Resolved that the sound of the magical words should not be lost, I rose from my chair with the intention of retrieving our audio recording device.

"No!" cried the Mambo, suddenly shaken from her trance.

"But I must record this," I insisted.

"You must *learn* it," the young woman countered forcefully. "Then I must sing the second chant while *you* sing the first. Record *that* if you want to."

Her reticence frustrated me. I desired to record all parts of the chant—the separate parts and then both of them sung together. However, I glanced over at the sickly Knecht, and he waved his hand to indicate that I should indulge the Mambo.

"Very well," I told her. "Begin again, and I shall attempt to learn the song."

The Mambo's eyes rolled back once more, and the horrible, guttural song recommenced. For several minutes, it remained an unintelligible cacophony. However, as time passed, I began to recognize phrases that recurred. I began to memorize them and sang along with the Mambo each time they came around. Before half of an hour had passed, I was singing along more often than not. After a full hour, I was copying the Mambo precisely. I even snapped my hands in perfect time to her own.

As our voices and hands fell into perfect synchronization, the Mambo stopped. She came out of her trance, and her eyes focused on mine once again.

"Good," she said softly. "*Very* good. You have learned it well. Now you shall sing it alone, and I shall sing the second chant on top of it."

"Very well," I said and began the series of guttural noises and clicks I had just memorized. As I did so, Knecht slowly rose and made his way back upstairs to fetch the recording device. Moments later, the Mambo began to sing the second part of the incantation—and my god!—though I would have deemed it impossible, it was even *more* guttural and gravelly sounding than the first! Had I not known better, I would have guessed the Mambo was imitating a large animal in the final stages of childbirth (or at least copulation).

As we sang our strange noises together, I began to notice an eerie organization to it. The Mambo was clearly timing her incantations to my own. There were moments where our two voices seemed to answer one another, like a conversation. At other moments, we spoke a phrase or made a sound identical—our voices melding as one—before once again diverging into horrible dissonance. We sang together in this manner for several minutes.

Moving very slowly under the weight of his fever, Inspector Knecht eventually returned with the recording device and set it next to us. With a ponderous hand, he adjusted the spools of tape and depressed the pertinent button to begin recording. At that very moment, the Mambo stopped her song.

She looked up at me and smiled an evil smile.

When it was clear she would sing no more, I stopped my chant as well.

"We are recording now," I pointed out to her, indicating the spools with my finger. "Please continue the song so we may preserve it . . . or have you forgotten what I said about your teeth and fingernails?"

She only smiled at me. It was a confident smile. The smile of one with secret knowledge.

"Continue the song!" I demanded. "I command you, in the name of the Third Reich, to continue the song!"

"Unnecessary," retorted the Mambo. "It has already been effective."

At this insolence, I rose from my chair and struck her across the face as hard as I could. (Though her hands were now free, she did not flinch or block my blow. I hit her powerfully in the cheek.)

"Continue the song, now!" I shouted.

She only smiled icily. I drew the Luger from my waistband. I fully extended my arm and pressed the barrel hard against her forehead.
"Continue!" I cried. "Continue the—"

And here I stopped, for the sound of an unexpected blow echoed across the room. It was as though something had been thrown hard against the shuttered window facing the field.

The Mambo's smile brightened.

Then—*kramm!*—the sound of another blow echoed off the window. Then a scraping sound. Then silence. Then a powerful blow again.

The Mambo threw back her head and laughed, exposing a row of glistening white teeth.

"I believe your guests have arrived," she said.

"What nonsense is this?" I asked. I stalked over to the window and threw open the shutter.

The sight that greeted me is difficult to describe.

I found myself staring into the face of a zombie. He was ancient, covered in mud, and missing his nose and teeth. He emitted a roar from lungs that had not drawn breath in many years. I involuntarily flinched away and discharged my weapon into the wall.

But that was not all that I saw.

Beyond the zombie, in the field, were many others like him. *A least a hundred.* All of them looked positively ancient—decades dead, at least. Some were so decayed and desiccated that it was hard to recognize their forms as human. Some crawled or scuttled on the ground like insects or crabs. Others slunk forward slowly, on legs stiff as stilts. They were deformed. They were horrible to behold. Each of them that could moan, moaned. Every single one of them had turned to face (or, in some horrible cases, "face") the house.

The ground on which they stood—formerly a placid field, empty and pristine—was now a mess of upturned earth. In a horrible shocking instant, it became clear to me that not only had our song awakened the dead, but that they had heard our siren call *whilst underneath the very earth itself*!

"Europeans are idiots, each in their own way . . . but you Nazis take the cake!" cried the Mambo gleefully, as if our dire predicament were only a joke to her.

I trained my Luger on the zombie in the window and fired several times into his head. He moaned and fell to the ground, unmoving. Another stepped up and took his place almost simultaneously.

"Only the world's biggest fools would choose the house next to the old Grangou burying ground in which to interrogate Mambos on the art of raising zombies!" the young woman cackled from behind me.

"That isn't helpful!" I shouted, and then emptied the Luger into the field of zombies. At least two others fell; but, again, more zombies quickly took their place. It was clear the house should soon be swarmed if I did not improve my firepower.

"Knecht!" I cried to my colleague. "Thank God you opened that crate! We must fetch those machine guns and grenades immediately."

Suddenly, behind me, I heard a door slam.

"Knecht?" I cried and swiveled around.

The inspector was still sitting at the foot of the stairs, looking more overcome by his fever than ever. With an effort that clearly required great exertion, he lifted his arm and pointed to the chair. It was now empty. The Mambo had apparently untied her legs whilst my back was turned, and had just run out of the house and into the forest. The door was still ajar.

I wondered for a moment if Knecht and I ought to follow her. I approached the half-open door, intending to stick my head out and look beyond. No sooner had I grasped the handle than a moldy, teetering zombie stuck his head around the corner. It had no eyes, but it clearly sensed my presence and snapped at me with a jaw full of crooked teeth.

I recoiled in horror, kicked the door shut, and locked the zombie outside.

"Knecht," I shouted, "we are under siege! Where have you put the crate of armaments?"

My fellow inspector, who seemed on the verge of passing out from weakness, managed to point to the room at the back of the house where he had made his office.

I bounded over to the little room and found the crate underneath a blanket. I grabbed one of the MP 40s and began shoving grenades and ammunition clips into each and every pocket (and even down my trousers).

"Gehrin," my colleague moaned from the other room. "I think they are breaking through the window."

I raced back to the front of the house to find that Knecht was not exaggerating. A whole platoon of zombies seemed to be gathered around the window overlooking the field. They had smashed the glass, broken through the storm shutters, and now several sets of flailing arms reached inside. The smashing glass and gnashing teeth were not the only noise they made. The zombies emitted low moans. Now and then, they almost seemed to form coherent words. It was profoundly unnerving.

I pulled out my submachine gun and began firing into the mass of arms and teeth. I uttered a war cry that I hoped was worthy of a man of the Reich and watched as my bullets riddled the wriggling zombies. I tried my best to aim for their heads, but the mass of body parts and limbs writhed and thrashed violently, making precise aiming a near-impossibility.

As you may be aware, my <u>Obergruppenführer</u>, the clip on an MP 40 exhausts itself after only a few seconds of constant fire. I was forced to expend several clips before I had pushed the crowd of zombies back enough that it felt safe to lob a grenade through the window.

"Take cover!" I cried to Inspector Knecht and flattened myself against the floor.

"You fool!" he coughed. "The walls of this house are far too thin for that."

No sooner had he issued his warning than the ensuing blast conspired to prove him right. The grenade detonated—handily dispatching the remaining platoon of zombies lurking just outside the window—and tore a man-sized hole in the side of the house.

Dirt and dust rained down for a moment, and then all was silent. I stood and inspected the hole. It did not seem possible to repair with any haste. Looking beyond it, I saw the pile of dead zombies I had just created, but also dozens more still lumbering toward the house from across the field.

"Damn and blast," I cried. "Now they will overrun us if they reach the house. We must not allow that to happen. I'm going up to the roof through the hatch in the second floor. My only hope is to pick them off before they reach the opening. Knecht, you must go to your office and bring me the rest of the ammunition and grenades!"

"I can hardly stand," Knecht protested.

"All the same, you must do it!" I called, racing past him up the stairs. "Think of the Führer and be inspired."

As quickly as I could, I raced to the attic of the two-story house and popped open the hatch that allowed for access to the roof. Luckily, the slope of the roof was quite gradual, allowing me to stand and balance myself easily. The moonlight revealed a field filled with lumbering zombies. I would have to eliminate them one by one.

Seeking to conserve ammunition, I began by throwing grenades at places on the field where the zombies were clustered. This produced good results. Whether the zombies were unaware of my grenades or simply did not care about them, they proved almost entirely incapable of evasive action. This made my work as easy as a soldier's training exercise. Again and again I threw the grenades at the stumbling worm-eaten corpses that groaned and gnashed their teeth. Again and again, they failed to take cover, and were blown apart. Limbs, heads, and (on occasion) entire zombies were lifted into the air by the force of the blasts, and they rained down upon the field.

This grenade lobbing was highly effective, but it was still a challenge to explode the zombies before they reached the house. The field was very large, and I could only throw the grenades thirty or forty yards without losing my footing under the force of the throw. (And I could not throw the grenades too close to the house, or, as we had just seen, the structure itself would be damaged in the blast). Sooner than I liked, I had thrown my last one. Where was Knecht?

"Knecht!" I called into the roof hatch as I prepared my submachine gun. "Come quickly with more grenades!"

I fell onto my stomach, extended the collapsible stock of the MP 40, and braced the weapon against the edge of the roof. I then fired several rounds at the zombies nearest the house. Hitting the slow-moving fellows was no problem, but it proved maddeningly difficult to achieve the head shots required to bring them down. My natural inclination was to aim for the torso. By correcting this, and seeking to aim only for the head, I often overshot the shambling corpses. In most cases, I expended *an entire clip of ammunition* in the course of bringing down a single zombie. This was no way to work.

I was quickly down to my final clip, and still no sign of Knecht.

I stared hard into the field, where many zombies remained upright. Should I begin shooting with my final clip, or should I wait before expending it? These walking dead showed no signs of stopping. If I did not do anything, they would soon start entering the first floor of our house.

Suddenly, I detected a slow, lumbering movement right below me. Assuming—in that startled instant—that a zombie had risen from the dirt at the foot of the house, I hastily turned my gun on it and loosed a single round. No sooner had I done so than I realized the figure was not a zombie but Inspector Knecht.

He dropped the ammunition in his hands and slowly crumpled to the earth.

"Knecht!" I cried.

He did not respond.

Abandoning my plan of a rooftop defense, I scuttled back through the hatch and raced down to the first floor of the house and leaped out of the grenade hole through which my colleague had stumbled. There I found Knecht, facedown in the soil. The ground beside him was littered with the grenades and clips he had been carrying. I took a knee beside him and flipped him over. He moaned.

It appeared that my shot had only nicked his leg.

"Knecht, can you walk?" I asked urgently. Zombies were approaching from several directions, some less than ten yards away.

"For you . . .," Knecht moaned and squirmed, attempting to gesture to the grenades and SMG clips he had carried. Obviously, I should never have sent him to fetch ammunition. How I regretted this horrible mistake!

I gathered as many of the grenades and clips as I could, and then I lifted Knecht over my shoulder (thank goodness he is a relatively light and wiry man). No sooner had I done so than a dusty zombie lumbered to within an arm's reach of us. I leveled the SMG at him and fired until his head disintegrated.

It was difficult to replace the clip while holding Knecht, so I set him back down. (He was close to babbling from the fever—and, doubtless too, from the stress of the attack—and seemed only marginally aware of what was happening to him.) No sooner had I replaced the clip (and was ready to once again hoist Inspector Knecht over my shoulder) than another zombie drew within ten feet of us. This time I was more careful with my ammunition and brought him down with a single blast to the forehead. Then another directly behind the first lumbered forward, and I laid him back to the earth in similar fashion. Then yet another.

It soon became clear that carrying Knecht back up to my rooftop perch would be a dangerous (and probably impossible) undertaking. In a trice, I decided to make my stand then and there, in front of the house.

The fighting that followed was long and exhausting. To the bats that occasionally passed overheard and looked down on the scene below, it must have appeared that the remaining zombies circled around me the way water circles around a drain. The walking dead men seldom moved in a straight line, but always they found a way to careen or corkscrew in my general direction. As they stumbled within my range, I dispatched each one as quickly and efficiently as I could. As the night wore on, spent clips littered the ground around me, and the bodies of the zombies encircled me from all directions.

Finally—in the culmination of an effort I do not overstate as nearly superhuman (for, as the Führer reminds us, we Aryans are supermen)—I dispatched the final zombie. It was a frail Haitian girl, teeth gnashing and eye sockets gaping obscenely. I shot her through the forehead with what was nearly my final bullet. The sun had just begun to rise.

Utterly exhausted, I fell cross-legged on the ground next to Knecht (who was nearly buried underneath dead zombies). I tried to work up the strength to enter the house and get a glass of water. I surveyed the empty field as I sat. Before, it had been as smooth and green as the pitch on a golf course.

Now it was a no-man's-land of muddy craters where the dead had risen from their slumbers and clawed up through the broken earth. Nothing moved on this strange, blasted moonscape. I was thankful—at least—for that.

Then, unexpectedly, something did.

At the far edge of the field—over a hundred yards away—I saw two humanoid shapes. I had not noticed them before because they were unmoving, but now they turned to face one another. I could not discern if they were zombies or humans. One was a smaller, lithe-looking black woman. She looked not entirely unlike the Mambo we had just met. The other was Caucasian and had a hulking, almost-planetary carriage that closely reminded me of Inspector Baedecker's.

I took up my SMG and readied myself for the eventuality of dispatching two more zombies. And yet the figures made no move to approach me. After seeming to converse for a few moments, they simply turned and walked away. In a moment, they passed over the horizon and were gone.

Thus concludes my account of our first successful participation in the creation of zombies.

While we were not able to record the dual-voiced song that seems to be the secret, we now understand that this auditory phenomenon is a salient part of the ceremony, and that the rest is, as they say, window dressing. The potential for weaponizing this in the cause of the Reich is grand indeed. I envision zeppelins—equipped with great loudspeakers— broadcasting the chants across enemy territory. (When our enemy's armies are exhausted from fighting their own dead, *then* we shall strike them with the full might of the Reich! In their weakened and spent conditions, we shall annihilate them utterly!)

I have been able—I believe—to perfectly recall my half of the guttural chant, which I have reproduced on the enclosed spool of tape. Given that we now know exactly what we are looking for, I am optimistic about our chances of quickly capturing a second Bocor/Mambo and inducing them to divulge the second voice for our recording device.

I am also happy to report that Inspector Knecht is making a slow but steady recovery from his tropical fever. He was well enough on the day after the events described to assist me as I dragged the dead zombies into a great pile and set them aflame.

Please find enclosed the spool of tape featuring my singing, as well as a request for a new shipment of munitions to the address provided.

Yours respectfully,
Oswaldt Gehrin

COMMUNICATION 22

June 2, 1940
From: Franz Baedecker
To: <u>Reinhard Heydrich</u>

My dear <u>Obergruppenführer</u>,

I am on the cusp of learning many, many wonderful things. More
reports soon to follow.

Respectfully,
Franz Baedecker

COMMUNICATION 23

June 5, 1940
From: Gunter Knecht
To: <u>Reinhard Heydrich</u>

<u>Obergruppenführer</u>,

I don't know.

I really just don't know.

As Gehrin may have informed you, I am on the mend after having succumbed to a noxious tropical fever. My symptoms included extreme weakness and frequent disorientation. Under the fever's burden, I often had difficulty understanding what was happening around me. My dreams felt more vivid and real than my waking moments. I suffered from extreme exhaustion and dehydration. And I was, I now believe, in a *highly* suggestible state.

At what am I hinting?

No, it is too fantastic to say directly. I must build my case brick by brick before proceeding to a closing argument.

Look back, dear <u>Obergruppenführer</u>, over each of my transmissions to you thus far. You will notice that whilst zombies are always uppermost in my thoughts—as they quite should be—I have *never, reported laying eyes upon one myself*.

Inspectors Gehrin (and previously Baedecker) have testified to me—as they doubtless have to you—that they have been in the direct presence of the walking dead on many occasions. They have seen animate zombies walking around, and even inter-acted with some of the walking dead. Indeed, most of my actions taken during this mission have been directly predicated by these zombie testimonials of my fellow inspectors.

However, let us now propose—at first, purely as an academic exercise—that zombies do not exist. That they are a Haitian folktale, or attributable entirely to some unremarkable and purely scientific expla-nation. (Perhaps Voodooists "create" zombies by giving a living person an extract from a plant that makes them *appear* momentarily dead, but from which they then recover, thus allowing the Bocor to claim to have "reanimated" them. It is unbelievably banal and disappointing, yes, but please indulge me for the sake of this argument.)

Now suppose that two RSHA agents have an interest in maintaining the illusion that zombies do exist. One of them, let us hypothetically allege, is lazy, corpulent, and feels as though the position of his family in the upper echelons of German society entitles him to a life free from hard work and responsibility. Suppose that another agent fancies himself a scientist and would like to position himself as an important researcher deserving of many honors, rewards, and sinecures after the war.

How would these agents conspire to execute such an illusion? Well, they might start by claiming to see zombies in many places, but always fail to bring back a specimen to verify their claims. *Some* "evidences" would no doubt be presented—totems, Voodoo dolls, "sacred" objects—but never a real zombie. These illusionists would also make contact with local Haitians and—probably through the use of bribes—employ them as actors in a grand play. Through carefully orchestrated encounters, the rogue RSHA agents would create situations in which their trusting colleague would always *just* miss the actual zombies, and yet others would corroborate their zombie claims. (I struggle, for example, to understand the young man with the cleft palate who abducted me, and the man of similar description who apparently misled Inspector Gehrin.)

But let us now consider the remarkable events during my fever.

What do I remember of Inspector Gehrin's sing-along with a Haitian woman and the ensuing "attack" on our home? Very little. In my fevered state, things seemed unreal, and my memory was not working correctly.

I can confirm that there is a great hole in the side of our house that Inspector Gehrin made with a Model 24 grenade. I can confirm that Inspector Gehrin and myself immolated approximately 150 rotting bodies (into which Gehrin had expended almost our entire reserve of ammunition). I can confirm that approximately 150 holes have appeared in the field adjacent to our house that were not there at the start of my fever.

This much is fact, and not opinion.

But as to the *events* of the night in question . . . Here it is a bit less cut-and-dried.

I have *some* vague recollection of Gehrin singing a horrible-sounding song with a young (and yes, quite comely) Haitian woman he called a/the Mambo. (I remember rising to fetch a tape recorder for them at one point.) I also recall the noise of someone banging upon the doors and windows on the outside of our home, and Gehrin's (and the Mambo's) insistence that zombies were now present. (Were they actual zombies, or were they only locals that Gehrin had paid to bang on the doors at an appointed time?)

I then recall Gehrin disappearing up to the roof and firing off half of our munitions, and then insisting that—even in my fevered state—I must bring him the second half. (This was an inappropriate request to make on a sickly person and may have put my health in critical danger). When I attempted to follow his instructions and bring him the weapons, the weight of the ammunition clips and grenades pushed my already-exhausted body into a state of mania. (Gehrin may have been counting on this.) I then vaguely recall wandering out through a hole in the wall of the house and collapsing under the weight of my load. When I awoke, Gehrin was standing next to me, and we were surrounded by a pile of disgusting, maggot-eaten corpses that Gehrin claimed to have "killed."

Indeed.

This "phenomenon" of zombies appearing only when I am absent or fevered beyond reason also proves true in my dealings with Father Gill. While he and his consortium of religious officials seemed to hint that zombies were real, none of them confirmed anything like the walking, ravenous corpses vouched for by Gehrin. Could Gill, like Gehrin, have an interest in deceiving me? Perhaps he sought to impress me with his expertise, in hopes that a Jesuitical recommendation might free him from his responsibilities in the country. Perhaps he is a homosexual—a group the Führer rightly lumps with Gypsies and Jews—and sought to seduce me through displaying a knowledge of zombies. (I *have* been described as a fine Aryan specimen.) Whether Gill's disappearance is by design—and the encounter at his zombie ceremony was as much a charade as Gehrin's—or whether he was the victim of a legitimate kidnapping is unknowable.

As I say, <u>Obergruppenführer</u>, I just don't know.

Faced with so many unnerving possibilities regarding the agents operating under me (and my contacts here in Haiti), I can only continue forward by reminding myself of my most fundamental precept: I am here to serve the best interests of the Reich.

I, of course, pray that my hunches are wrong, and that a weaponizable version of aggressive zombies will yet be discovered and easily replicated. If, however, I can prove that my hunches are right, I, intend to see that Inspector Gehrin (and Baedecker, if I can find him) are sent back to Berlin and brought up on charges. (Given that we are in a state of war, I do not see how wasting the Reich's time and resources can constitute anything less than treason.)

As we continue our research here, I intend to shadow Gehrin without his knowledge, and to discover the truth.

Respectfully,
Gunter Knecht

COMMUNICATION 24

June 15, 1940
From: Gunter Knecht
To: Reinhard Heydrich

Obergruppenführer,

I am in receipt of your communication.

I apologize if my previous missive was inappropriately personal. I sought only to convey my frustrations that our predicaments here have not yet resulted in information that can be of use. If you came away with the impression that I am (as you put it) "paralyzed" or "incapable of maintaining strong leadership" over the RSHA officers subordinate to me, then I have done a poor job of communicating the situation. I assure you—in the strongest possible terms—that there is no need to relieve me of my duties. I am in full control of the situation, and no person in the entire Reich is more committed to our cause, or more capable, than myself.

I was, of course, surprised to learn that Inspector Baedecker is not dead, and that—further—he is still in communication with you. (I assume, however, that you are not in communication with him, correct?

Though our encrypted letters may be dropped at any of the U-boat collection points around the country, I understand that you will only communicate directly with our headquarters.)

The notion that Baedecker was present at—or even *supervised*—the (purported) zombie attack upon our position is deeply troubling. (Do you mean to say that he was the one who banged on the windows and doors during Gehrin's strange opera? Or did he somehow oversee the zombies?)

As you mandate, we shall reestablish communication with him as soon as possible and extract from him what information he has learned.

My strength now fully restored, I undertook an interrogation of Inspector Gehrin shortly after sending you my last letter. He objected to this quite vociferously and repeatedly declared that his accounts of zombies have always been true and factual. I can report that his story stayed consistent through several hours of interrogation involving both physical and mechanical components. (It is never pleasant to interrogate a fellow German—much less a fellow member of the RSHA—but I reminded myself that a true servant of the Reich should have nothing to fear. And anyhow, as I assured Gehrin, the swelling in his testicles should subside in a matter of days, and the bruising is largely limited to his torso, where it is unlikely to be noticed.)

In light of his insistence that zombies are not the product of his own manufacturing or imagination, I have ordered Gehrin to resume his fieldwork. However, he now understands that his single and primary function is to acquire a "living" zombie. This will prove to me that the zombies are, in fact, real (and also then provide a specimen for vivisection, which, in my opinion, should be the next step in our work).

Whatever ends up being the fruit of our efforts in this country, I hope it is clear to you that I have always sought to comport myself with the best interests of the Reich in mind. I still firmly believe that my colleagues cannot say as much.

Respectfully,
Gunter Knecht

Postscript: Radio broadcasts indicate that we have taken Paris. Is there anyone left who still doubts the might and majesty of the Reich? London shall be next, of course.

COMMUNICATION 25

June 22, 1940
From: Oswaldt Gehrin
To: Reinhard Heydrich

My Obergruppenführer,

Extreme situations call for extreme measures.

In the history of scientific progress, the greatest leaps forward have often been made through undertakings that involved danger—be it to the scientist's reputation or to his very physical safety. One recalls Galileo's research into the earth's rotation around the sun—for which he knew he would be persecuted and prosecuted by the church. Did this deter the great man? No, it did not. He knew the results of his work would be worth any reciprocity from the ignorant.

Germany's own Otto Lilienthal was killed by his own "hanged glider" when a crash destroyed his spine. His final words? "Small sacrifices must be made." How right he was. Scientists must sacrifice for the good of humanity. (And now we have only to look to the current war to see applications of his glider in furthering the cause of our great nation.)

And one needs only the smallest inventiveness to picture the grim history of dangerous medical surgeries that have allowed for the precise operations that doctors can perform today.

So now, my <u>Obergruppenführer</u>, it is the same spirit that propelled these scientific luminaries forward that now moves me to dedicate myself more completely to the task at hand.

Two things have conspired to make this more complete dedication possible. The first is that Inspector Knecht has gone absolutely insane.

Incredibly, after my heroic defense of our headquarters *and his own person* against an overwhelming zombie attack, Inspector Knecht accused me of having fabricated the entire episode. He went on to say he doubted the veracity of the many corroborated field reports involving zombies I had made to him. Knecht insisted I submit to an interrogation—to which, as a dutiful servant of the Reich, I agreed. Even under the application of substantial physical discomfort, I consistently recalled every detail of my encounters with zombies and insisted upon their veracity. And Knecht *still* seemed unconvinced, ordering me to recover a zombie and insisting that henceforward none of my reports of zombie activity shall be credited as true unless I can produce the zombie itself.

From where this paranoid state derives, I cannot know. Suffice to say, working with him has become intolerable.

This would quickly become an ongoing problem, were it not for the second thing that has redoubled my dedication to jump into my research with both feet.

After submitting to Knecht's incredibly unpleasant—and, I hope you will agree, superfluous—interrogation, I was ordered to resume my search for zombies. It was with no little resentment toward him that I stalked once again into the moonlit jungles to troll for more members of the walking dead.

For a few days, all of my leads were cold. The usual hunting grounds near Bell's Hill proved entirely bereft of Voodoo activity, and the ceremonial clearing where Baedecker had been abducted proved empty (and appeared to have been unused for some time). Additional attempts to encounter zombies or Voodooists in other locations were likewise fruitless. (This failure, as you may imagine, only added to Knecht's paranoid delusions that zombies do not exist, and that I sought to perpetrate some manner of hoax suggesting otherwise.)

Then after nearly a week of fruitless search, it happened.

Whilst stalking through the Haitian wilds—fearing bandits and despairing that perhaps I should never find another zombie—I suddenly saw exactly what I was looking for. A lone, unattended zombie—neither too young and fresh, or too rotting and decomposed—toddled down the forest path and then ran past my hiding spot. When I was sure it was quite alone, I sprang from my place of concealment and threw a rope with a sliding noose around it. In a trice, I tightened the noose and pinned the zombie's arms to its sides. However, it began to fight back. Even with its arms tied, it proved a dangerous opponent.

The zombie gnashed its teeth manically and thrust itself toward me, attempting to bite me anywhere it could. (I instantly regretted not having lassoed its legs; tripping it would have proven much more useful.) The fellow was relentless. After a few moments of struggle, a booming—and familiar—voice echoed through the forest around me. The zombie fell motionless to the ground, and Inspector Baedecker stepped out of the underbrush.

"Watch yourself, Gehrin," Baedecker said. "A single bite from a zombie can slowly turn you into a member of the walking dead yourself. You and Knecht—and your 'research'—have likely missed this important fact."

"Baedecker!" I cried. "What has happened to you?"

For indeed, the sight of Baedecker was not nearly as surprising as the figure he now presented. While still very large, it was obvious that time in the forest had given him a slightly leaner aspect. His costume also featured new adornments in the forms of feathers, plants, and written decorations. Several wooden amulets dangled from his fleshy neck and clacked when he walked. His face was decorated with paints as I have seen in renderings of the American Indians.

"I have been admitted to an inner circle, allowing me to pursue a more intimate study of the zombie," Baedecker replied. "And our meeting tonight is not an accident. After some consideration, I have chosen to admit you to that circle as well."

"What happened to you?" I asked, befuddled. "The last time I saw you, you were being abducted by zombies!"

"I was not abducted," Baedecker said. "I allowed myself to be selected."

"What do you mean?" I asked.

"Do you recall the night when we discovered the Voodoo ceremony and you were knocked unconscious?" he asked. "I must now confess that it was I who delivered that blow."

"Why, whatever for?" I asked, dumbfounded.

"Because I had peered into their camp—and I knew that I must come to the Voodooists *alone*," he answered. "You are basically a capable man, Inspector Gehrin, but as soon as my brain processed the importance of what I was seeing, I knew with all conviction that I must come to it without you."

"I see," I answered cautiously.

"While you were lying on the forest floor, I entered that clearing of wild revelry and introduced myself to the Voodooists," said Baedecker. "They showed me wonderful things. Amazing things! Some of which I still do not fully understand. Then they invited me to join them. Eventually, I elected to do so. I could not leave with them that night—

improperly equipped and provisioned as I was—but I made it clear to the Voodooists that they should expect me in the near future. It was a ruse when I 'awoke' next to you the following morning. I apologize for tricking you, but I hope you see that it was necessary."

"Where exactly have you been all this time?" I asked. "Knecht and I assumed you had been killed."

"First of all, Knecht is a fool and an imbecile," Baedecker asserted. "His shortsightedness threatens to disrupt any chance we have of making progress here that will sincerely benefit the Reich."

"I must confess, I am pleased to hear you still hold allegiance to the Reich," I told him. "I quite feared that you had 'gone native' entirely and abandoned your Aryan brothers for a life among the Voodooists."

"Hardly," he replied with a chuckle. "By streamlining my research—and sloughing off the yoke of that idiot Knecht—I have accomplished in a matter of months what might have otherwise taken years."

Here, I found I could not contain my own anger at Inspector Knecht and gushingly recounted for Baedecker the details of my capture of a Mambo, my earnest attempts to protect

Knecht from the attacking zombies, and the cruel interrogation with which I was rewarded.

"Yes, you should not have kidnapped that Mambo," Baedecker said flatly. "However, I must admit that I was impressed to learn you participated in the Song of the Jeje. It is the rite by which zombies are created."

"I know. It was remarkable!" I said. "And still, the fool Knecht did not believe me! He claimed it was all a ruse to disturb his fevered mind. The very absurdity!"

Then as patriotism coursed through me, I added, "And just think of the applications for war in the European theater!"

"Yes," said Baedecker. "But you must think more broadly still. Forcing our enemies to fight against a zombie horde is a good thing, but it is not everything. Our leader has said that the Reich will last for a thousand years. By discovering the secrets of the Voodooists, perhaps the Führer himself will be so long lasting."

"What do you mean?" I asked.

"Only that the Haitians have hit upon the ancient secret to reanimating the dead but lack the ambition to use it for anything other than a religious ceremony producing indentured servants. Imagine what this technology can do in the hands of an ambitious race like our own! When the secrets of zombies are rightly purposed and refined, we may yet kill death itself!"

"But . . . ," I stammered, "the Führer as a zombie—while an undeniably interesting notion—seems an unsatisfying tribute to the man. Would it not dishonor our great leader to turn him into one of these shambling, bloodthirsty abominations?"

"Bah!" spat Baedecker. "These Haitians in their mud huts can only bring back a man as a monster. But imagine what Germans in laboratories can do! Once we have the core of their technology—which appears to be entirely auditory—we may be able to refine it until our zombies are simply men, fully reincarnated and reanimated."

"I believe I follow you," I said. "And if we could do that, then yes, perhaps we *could* kill death itself! It is at least worth pursuing."

"I knew that you would agree," Baedecker said. "That is why I have decided that now is the time to reach out to you and invite you to join my independent research. During this time away, I have been living exclusively among the Voodooists. I take part in their rituals, I listen to the words of their leaders, and—as you see—I have even been entrusted with zombies."

"And you are not tempted to vivisect them—the zombies, I mean?" I asked. "As a man of science, you must long to see your questions answered. I often have wondered how zombies will react when limbs are removed, for example."

"Yes, I am tempted," Baedecker said. "Do not let my costume fool you. I live with the Voodooists, share in their customs, and eat their calorically unsatisfying meals—but that does not mean I have forgotten the precepts of science. Yet by positioning myself as a willing acolyte, I am gradually being indoctrinated more and more deeply into their world. As you see, I have already learned the tricks and utterances that can render an otherwise-bloodthirsty zombie harmless."

He motioned to the lassoed zombie still lying at our feet like a becalmed canine.

"I believe that if we can pool our knowledge and resources, the Reich may live for a thousand years in a *very* literal sense," he said.

As you can see, my <u>Obergruppenführer</u>, Inspector Baedecker presents a very compelling case. Thus, I have agreed to join him in his intimate research among the Voodooists. I am writing this missive from Baedecker's new headquarters, a modest dwelling deep in the forest on the outermost edge of a small encampment of Voodoo faithful. I am fully aware that Inspector Knecht may not approve of the approach we intend to pursue. Therefore, I have made no attempt to notify him of our activities. I will continue to send you field reports as opportunities warrant, but will be unable to receive communication from you, obviously.

With any luck, we shall soon emerge from this dark place with information that has the potential to change the course of European history—if not human history—forever.

Despite this detour from procedure, we remain your obedient servants.

Yours respectfully,
Oswaldt Gehrin

COMMUNICATION 26

June 26, 1940
From: Gunter Knecht
To: Reinhard Heydrich

Obergruppenführer,

Lying and calumny!

Just as I sit down to write you a letter detailing the disappearance of Inspector Gehrin, I receive word from you that he has abandoned his post and joined Baedecker in an unauthorized investigation beyond my auspices as the supervising RSHA officer. This is beyond imagining!

This dire situation calls for plain speaking. I see only a few likely possibilities:

Baedecker (perhaps swayed by Voodooists) has captured Gehrin.

Baedecker and Gehrin *have* discovered Voodoo secrets and wish to study them without supervision so they may steal them and use them for personal gain. (Again, I find this questionable, as I still have not seen compelling evidence that zombies exist.)

Baedecker and Gehrin have abandoned their posts out of cowardice, a preference for life in a tropical country, a dislike of the RSHA command structure, or other reasons. (I find this scenario *most* likely.),

In any of the above cases, it follows that Inspector Baedecker (and very probably Inspector Gehrin) must be executed as traitors.

Treason against one's nation is punishable by death. So is abandoning one' soldierly post in a time of war. In the very least, these men have abandoned their posts. It would be within my purview to punish them accordingly. More troubling—though in my opinion less likely—is the idea that they may soon be in possession of knowledge that would have military value to the Reich. Obviously, I must not allow this knowledge—if it even exists—to fall into the wrong hands.

I understand that Baedecker and Gehrin are still in communication with you, Obergruppenführer. Thus I urge you to advise our U-boat teams to set up watches at the drop points. When they attempt to communicate again, they may thus be apprehended.

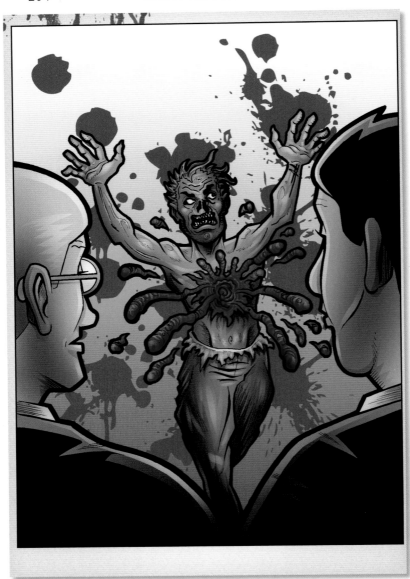

In the meantime, you can be assured that I shall not rest until these two scoundrels have been captured or killed. (I know you would expect nothing less of me.) Before they die, I shall wrest from them any secrets they have learned and make them known to you.

Respectfully,
Gunter Knecht

COMMUNICATION 27

June 29, 1940
From: Oswaldt Gehrin
To: Reinhard Heydrich

My Obergruppenführer,

Since taking up residence with Inspector Baedecker in the Voodooist settlement, I have witnessed many strange and exotic rituals—the majority of which I have not the time or space to limn here. However, I have twice witnessed the Song of the Jeje used to raise zombies. It has proven itself to be the same song that I sang in the presence of the Mambo.

The village is a small one, though its character varies greatly depending on the time of day. Any traveler discovering it during daylight hours will see a modest collection of fifteen or so homes and a population apparently engaged in subsistence farming. By night, however, the encampment comes alive with bonfires, singing, drumming, and dancing. The population seems to triple or quadruple; and men, women, and children engage in all manners of rituals, cavorting, and worship—often until the dawn's first light. In this dark nocturnal carnival, I have seen things that I never would have credited as possible.

I have seen a wild pig emerge from the forest walking on two legs and seemingly converse with humans who knew it as a friend. I have seen ghostly apparitions with human forms appear at the edges of the Voodoo gatherings and then melt back into nothing. (They leave behind a strange, ethereal mucus on the trees.) I have seen a circle of Voodooists seem to levitate six feet off the ground as they chanted and sang—seemingly unaware that this was an unusual consequence of chanting.

If anything, dear Obergruppenführer, the wonders and powers of the Voodooists have been *under*reported in the Western world.

There is a hierarchy to the structure of the Voodoo practitioners here, and it is more complicated (and involves more subtlety) than a casual observer might give it credit. Yet there can be no question that it is an ancient, wizened Bocor who occupies the central position in the group's power structure. The man—his name is Grandmarnier—is reputed to be 102 years old (though he looks perhaps sixty). He is also said to be able to change his appearance through sheer force of will and sometimes appears older or younger. I have not yet seen this feat accomplished, though I *have* seen the man raise zombies.

(In connection to this presumed agelessness of Grandmarnier, Inspector Baedecker remains convinced that the ultimate value of our discoveries may be a means of preserving life indefinitely. It is his hope that through scientific refinement, the Reich will be able to reanimate its members as fully sentient zombies, with little or no taste for flesh. I do not disagree that this is an admirable goal, however lofty, yet I continue to see a more immediate value in the creation of murderous zombies for use in the European conflict.)

Grandmarnier appears to have taken a particular shine to Inspector Baedecker. I do not know what actions—taken prior to my arrival—fostered such a wealth of good feeling between the two men, but it cannot be denied. And upon Baedecker's vouching for me, I have also been accepted, though somewhat more hesitantly, into a circle of trust. The Voodooists seem completely unaware that we intend to use their rituals for military purposes. Neither Baedecker

nor I have given them any impression that this is the case. (Following Baedecker's lead, I have presented myself as a European with a wanderlust, keen to find a more "authentic" and "natural" way of living. I give no hint that I am aware of the practical applications for their technologies.)

Grandmarnier, like the rest of the Voodooists in this cloistered village, does not seem to regard his powers as supernatural and exotic—or even as unusual. Great secrets for controlling the natural world are tossed about as though they were mere trifles or magician's tricks. (Further, he is keen to share them with willing acolytes.)

Thus, the most exciting news: Grandmarnier has agreed to teach us the second voice in the Song of the Jeje. (I am relearning the part I sang that ominous evening with the Mambo, and Baedecker is learning the Mambo's part.) Obviously, this is momentous, because it will allow us to create zombies on our own. Though the song is onerous and complicated, I believe we will have it mastered within hours of Grandmarnier delivering the lesson. At such time, the correct course of action will probably be to connect with one of our U-boat teams and return to Germany (where the song can be recorded, analyzed, and utilized as our glorious leaders see fit).

I feel we are close to success, my Obergruppenführer, and your helpful guidance has been the force behind our accomplishments here. Upon our return to Germany, we shall make clear to everyone that you are the one who deserves credit for this valuable discovery that shall so greatly strengthen the Reich.

Yours respectfully,
Oswaldt Gehrin

COMMUNICATION 28

June 30, 1940
From: Gunter Knecht
To: <u>Reinhard Heydrich</u>

<u>Obergruppenführer</u>,

I am in receipt of your letter detailing the communication you received from Gehrin and Baedecker. (How cunning of them to send an innocent Haitian child to the drop point as their deliveryman. I see that, even under the harshest interrogation by the U-boat crew, he was unable to divulge the whereabouts of the inspectors in question, or the location of the settlement they inhabit.)

I am, however, alarmed by your inclination to believe its contents.

My <u>Obergruppenführer</u>, Gehrin and Baedecker are deceivers and traitors. Your instructions to me—to allow them to proceed in their studies unmolested—only attest to their powers of deception! During their time here in Haiti, the scope of their lies has gradually grown larger and larger. Now they deceive even you! That they should now dangle a plethora of supernatural discoveries in front of your nose evinces only that they are making this up as they go along. Whatever their motivations, Gehrin and Baedecker do not serve the best interests of the Reich. The abandonment of their posts is inexcusable, as is nearly every other action they have taken.

My attempts to locate Gehrin and Baedecker—though so far unsuccessful—will continue. I shall search every inch of this blasted heath of a country if necessary! When I do locate them, they shall pay the ultimate price for their trespasses.

Respectfully,
Gunter Knecht

COMMUNICATION 29

July 1, 1940
From: Gunter Knecht
To: <u>Reinhard Heydrich</u>

<u>Obergruppenführer</u>,

While it is Baedecker and Gehrin who claim to be in touch with supernatural powers, allow me now to perform some epistolary prestidigitation that will have all the seeming of a psychic ability.

You, Reinhard Heydrich, are familiar with my dossier and my record of service to the Reich. However, you are ignorant of the *precise* details of my participation in Operation Zendor—an espionage initiative conducted along the Polish border directly prior to my assignment to Haiti.

Now I cup my ear. Even from thousands of miles away, I hear you opening my file and flipping through the pages. How does that final entry on my little CV go? Something like

Operation Zendor—A covert action involving top-secret SD/RSHA agents designed to provoke hostilities on the part of Polish forces along the border (allowing Germany to then "defend itself" against

Polish aggressors). Inspector Knecht was the ranking operative, and though the other members of his squad were lost to a Polish counterattack (which, in and of itself, qualifies the operation as successful), he received numerous citations for bravery and exemplary service to the Reich.

Yes, well and good. And accurate . . . to a point. But not complete. This account leaves out the details of the snowy evening on which the Polish security services tracked down the location of our headquarters (it was near Piasek), from whence we carried out our campaign of sabotage and murder.

Of all the things it could have been, it was a stray dog that saved my life that night.

It had been rummaging through our garbage for scraps for several nights in a row, creating, I felt, an unsupportable distraction. On the night in question, I saw it approach and chased it into the snowy fields that abutted the sizable farmhouse that was our home. The dog was cunning, but I more so. Within the hour, I had found its den and slit its throat. (Its pups I merely squashed with the heel of my boot.) I then beat a happy retreat back to the farmhouse, eager to tell my colleagues that the hungry cur would trouble us no longer. Yet the moment the house came into sight, all of my training told me something was not right.

True, the plume of healthy blue smoke still puffed, from the crumbling stone chimney, and the candles on the kitchen table still flickered brightly through the front windows. Yet things were still amiss. Things that only the most superior RSHA operative would notice.

I noticed the storm cellar door, now slightly ajar. I noticed the tracks in the snow made by alien boots, heavy and not of German issue. I noticed the unnatural stillness that had overtaken the house, as though my fellow agents—still, presumably, inside—were making a point of remaining unseen.

It wasn't much, but it was enough. Enough to tell me something was wrong.

Accordingly, I stayed concealed in the fields and waited for night to fall. When it was dark enough, I crept to the side of the house and set it afire. I shot down the Polish agents, one by one, as they fled the smoke and flames through the doors and (later) the windows. Afterward, in the basement cellar, I found the bodies of my fellow RSHA agents, now charred almost beyond recognition. How the Poles had found us—and how they had known to lie in wait for me—was not something I ever discovered. But as my dossier should show, the mission was ultimately counted a success.

Now . . .

I gather that these added details—attesting to my acumen in the field—might have "informed" (or even, dare I say, "altered completely") your decision to send a U-boat crew ashore with orders to assassinate me. Our U-boats are rightly known as the terrors of the sea. The sailors who man them are stalwart fellows—experts in their work—and just as dedicated to the Reich as you or I. But let us be honest—they are not trained to operate on land. The "trap" they laid for me made that perfectly clear.

It was a scenario oddly similar to what I encountered in Poland. I was returning home from yet another fruitless night spent in search of Gehrin and Baedecker. It was about six in the morning. When the house (with its adjacent pile of immolated corpses) came into view, it was obvious that a man was lying in wait for me on the roof. His attempts to conceal himself with a cluster of branches and leaves—that would otherwise never have been present on the roof—made this painfully clear. A moment's further surveillance revealed the other crewmen waiting for me inside the hole made by Gehrin's grenade.

While it would have been fairly easy to repeat the tactic I used in Poland—and immolate the U-boat crew—there were many valuable possessions still inside the house (not the least, as you can see, my encryption machine, which I am using to render this letter secure). Thus, I waited for one of the crew to relieve himself in the woods. After slitting his throat with a knife, I donned his uniform and returned to the house. I did not resemble the man physically, but the uniform allowed me to get very close to his fellow crewmembers before they realized something was wrong. By that time, I dispatched them handily with my Luger.

And so . . .

As you will have surmised, I am writing this from an undisclosed location. I will not make my whereabouts known to you until I have captured or killed Agents Gehrin and Baedecker (and learned whatever purported Voodoo secrets they possess). You needn't waste the Reich's time and expense by sending another U-boat crew to the house. I have removed all weapons and anything else salient to the mission.

In the history of heroic and patriotic accomplishment, there is a tradition of the "outlaw," who must, for a time, be exiled from his or her cause in order to eventually serve it with optimum effectiveness. It is into that tradition that I now boldly step.

You may rest assured, my Obergruppenführer, that when all of this is over, there will be no enmity between us. This attempt you have made on my life (and any subsequent) shall be regarded as the smallest tiff between close brothers.

I remain your obedient servant.

Respectfully,
Gunter Knecht

Postscript: In the event I choose to continue to communicate with you, I will—like Gehrin and Baedecker—use proxies to deliver my messages. They will not know who I am, or where I reside. You may interrogate them if you wish, but be assured you will learn nothing. Finally, let me point out that a further review of my dossier should establish that I am quite skilled in jungle survival and an expert in operating covertly for extended periods of time. I hope this will dissuade you from sending any other operatives of the Reich to capture or kill me. In the unlikely event they do find me, they will also find death. Of that you may be very certain.

COMMUNICATION 30

July 1, 1940
From: Oswaldt Gehrin
To: <u>Reinhard Heydrich</u>

My <u>Obergruppenführer</u>,

Our successes compound!

Under the tutelage of Grandmarnier, the Song of the Jeje is now perfected! Inspector Baedecker and I have mastered the ritual. How it works is still largely unknown to me, but I can attest that it *does* work. And with the permission of Grandmarnier, Baedecker and I have raised a zombie! (Baedecker has jocularly christened him Hans, after a primary school classmate he apparently resembles.)

Using a corpse procured from a burial ground several miles away, we performed the song on a starless night in a clearing lit only with torches. At my own suggestion, we sought to use this ritual to distill the Voodoo down to its most essential (and functional) elements. Thus, we commenced the song with none of the decoration or affectation of the traditional Voodooist. Only the song was used. The corpse was placed on the bare ground before us. Drums, feathers, and ceremonial garb were not employed.

Yet much to our delight, it was still effective! When the song was through, the fingers of the corpse began to twitch. Moments later, the thing sat up and looked at us. There was comprehension in its eyes as its gaze met our own. Baedecker and I were jubilant.

"We have done it!" Baedecker cried and began to dance a happy jig, right there on the jungle floor.

The result was near disaster.

For in the midst of his dance of joy, Baedecker—you will remember that he is an awkward and overweight man— slipped on a root and hit his head on the side of a tree, falling unconscious.

Zombies, as I hope I have made clear at this point, are slavering and innately violent creatures. They want nothing more than to eat human brains. They can, however, be controlled and rendered relatively docile through the use of certain powerful (dare I say magical?) words. (Other things, too, seem to have this ability. Certain drums can attract zombies like a homing beacon. Certain signals and mark-ings do not divest a zombie of its aggressive aspect, but they nonetheless protect the wearer from the zombie. We are learning much. It is fascinating!)

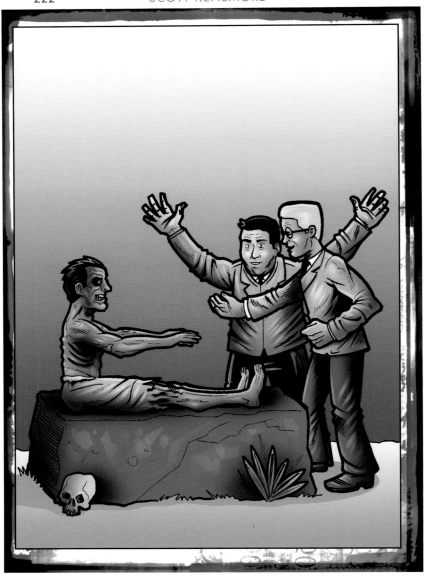

It was these very magical words (already taught to Baedecker by Grandmarnier) that he intended to share with me after our animation of the zombie.

As Baedecker lay prostrate on the ground beside me, Hans rose to his feet with a murderous look in his rolling yellow eyes. His teeth began to grind, and he extended his arms like a blind man feeling his way forward.

"Baedecker!" I cried, but my colleague was surely unconscious.

The murderous zombie began to stumble forward.

"Stop!" I cried, a great fear coursing through me. "I am the one who has created you. You must respect me!"

Yet alas, Hans did no such thing. Onward he came, his hands—they seemed more like claws—snatching violently at the air.

As our ritual was to be a scientific exercise conducted in relative safety, I had not brought my Luger. As Hans drew nearer—his grave breath cold and stinking—I prepared to flee. But of course that would mean disaster! While I might easily elude the stumbling zombie, it should surely then turn its attention to Baedecker. Both my colleague and the valuable knowledge he carried would be lost.

Suddenly, as the zombie's yawning mouth drew near, I heard a strange voice deliver a familiar-sounding utterance of the Voodooists. The zombie collapsed unmoving at my feet.

I looked over at Baedecker. But no! He was still unconscious—his breathing visible, but only just. Someone else had spoken!

Looking around wildly, I detected a shadowy figure half concealed by the darkness. He stood at the clearing's edge opposite me. I could not make out his features in the flickering torchlight, but he wore the black clothes and collar of a man of the cloth.

It is Knecht, come to kill us! I thought to myself, and my blood ran cold anew.

But then the figure edged forward into the torchlight, and I beheld a visage entirely unknown to me. He was an older man with silver hair. He bore the ruddy signs of drink upon his cheeks. In addition to his clerical collar, he wore the clanking ebon necklaces of a Voodooist (nearly concealed— black on black—against his dark clothes).

"Who are you?" I asked anxiously.

"A loyal servant of the Voudun," the man answered in a thick Irish brogue. "*You*, my friend, cannot say the same."

"What?" I responded, but the man put up his hand to stay me.

"Let me save you some time," he continued. "My name is Father Gill. Your colleague—who I sincerely hope is now dead or back in Germany—would likely have spoken to you about me."

"Oh . . . ," I said, genuinely baffled. "He did speak of you. But . . . but . . ."

"Let me save you some more time," said Gill, again raising his hand. "You are German operatives, sent here to learn the secrets of Voodoo—like the French before you, and the many, many others before them."

"And you are a supporter of that gangster Churchill, I suppose," I answered defensively. "I fail to see why you people insist on meddling in Continental affairs! My nation has only ever acted defensively!"

"Save your patriotic speeches, for I care not a whit for Churchill or Chamberlain," seethed my guest. (His tone was aggressive and curt.) "It matters not from what nation you people come. The fact that you are here to steal as your spoils the secrets of the Voodoo religion is the only matter of consequence. I offer you one choice, and one alone: Leave here this instant, return to your homeland, and speak nothing of what you have learned."

"You cannot be serious," I answered. "You are a man of the cloth. Knecht, before his insanity, told me of your mission to convert those *away* from the Voodoo faith toward the religions of Europe!"

"A necessary ruse," replied Gill. "It is true that I came here as a servant of the Catholic Church to convert the heathens, but it was *I* who was converted. Now I use my position under the Pope only to protect the country's native religion from missionaries and other interests. I am a member of a sizable—though necessarily secret—confederacy, and we are committed to preventing the exploitation of Voodoo secrets by sniveling outsiders."

"So then . . . ," I began.

"I could tell right away that your colleague was not all that he seemed," Gill continued. "Yes, he had researched his cover story well, but I have seen so many interlopers over the years that they have become easy to spot. At first, I tried to convince him that there was nothing to see. When he would not believe me (perhaps because of things he—or, come to think of it, *you*—observed), I tried to make it clear to him that investigating the Voodooists any further would be dangerous to his person. Perhaps he told you of the ritual I took him to—completely staged, of course—at which I fed him incorrect information about how zombies are created, and then gave him the impression that his own life was in danger."

"He did," I said, thinking on it.

"In retrospect, it would have been easier to have killed him," Gill explained. "Of course, that would only have prompted your government to send others to take his place. The only satisfactory resolution is always to convince interlopers that

there is nothing to find, or to send them in the wrong direction entirely. Of course, I did not know how much Knecht
knew. Had he heard of Grandmarnier? Had he seen actual
zombies? Based on my educated guesses, I think I did a
very good job designing my charade."

"Did you know about us?" I stammered, pointing to myself
and Baedecker.

"Yes, I was made aware of Knecht's colleagues, who I
assume are the two of you," Gill answered coolly. "I gave
instructions that I thought would culminate in either your
leaving the country or your outright deaths. And yet, I see
that you are here, and still alive."

"Who are you to speak for the Voodooists?" I asked forcefully, my shock changing to rage. "Grandmarnier has
personally invited us to become his acolytes and has freely
shown us how to use his arts to raise zombies. Who are
you to keep us from his secrets?"

"Grandmarnier is as ignorant as he is powerful," Gill
declared. "He does not understand that Voodoo's powers
are in danger of exploitation by evil men. He has no experience of the world outside of this tiny country. Types such
as yourselves would use his secrets for your own gain—
perverting and distorting the magic he freely teaches. You
are here because you dream of creating an army of invin-

cible zombie soldiers to serve your leader with the ridiculous toothbrush mustache. Do you deny it, sir? I know it is the truth!"

I opened my mouth, but nothing came out.

"This is about more than who rules Europe for the next thirty years," said Gill. "This is about the most ancient secrets men ever stole from gods. Yes, *gods*! And if you will not swear, this instant, to abandon your plundering and leave here forever, then we have nothing more to say to one another."

Here my anger became uncontainable. Not only did this man—whoever he truly was—stand in the way of our valuable mission, he had *insulted the Führer's mustache*.

It could not stand.

"You are a damned fool if you think the secrets of zombie creation are for you alone!" I spat. "The Third Reich is the greatest entity ever known to man! It is for the Reich—and the Reich alone—to determine the best use for zombies."

"Then I see you have made your choice," Gill responded coldly, and in the same instant drew a Colt revolver from his pocket and leveled it at me. "Like all men who have sought to steal the secrets of Voodoo, you shall meet the end that you deserve!"

Before I could think, there was a deafening report . . . yet it was Gill who dropped to the ground dead!

I looked over and saw the reclining Inspector Baedecker holding his Luger, the smoke from its barrel mixing with the omnipresent smoke from the torches.

"Baedecker, you came to!" I stammered.

"And just in time," he replied, slowly rising to his feet. "That man was a fool, but a dangerous one. He shows how determined our enemies are to stop us."

In a few moments, Baedecker had recovered completely from his fall. Without further word about the interloping priest, Baedecker began his tutorial for me on the verbal control of a zombie.

As I write this letter, Hans the zombie is sitting at my feet, as tame as a kitten. Yet were I to utter the right set of syllables, he would become as murderous as a homicidal maniac. It is a strange feeling to have such complete and utter power over so potentially deadly a thing. Imagine the feeling of a lion tamer . . . but no, that is inadequate. (Though lions can be tamed, the tamer must never let his guard down, lest he be surprised. Further, the lion must be carefully coached for months or years to respond correctly to a tamer's whip.) Imagine the feeling of an inventor who has constructed the perfectly obedient and deadly automaton—yes, that is it precisely—and you have perhaps some notion of the sentiment that runs through my veins. I can loose the zombie on my enemies, and it will bite and claw until my foes' brains are eaten and the zombie sated. I can rest it by the door to my hovel, where it will stand as a trusted sentry. Or I can command it to stand in the corner and stare at the wall for hours on end if doing so should somehow benefit me. (And for all of these tasks, no training on the zombie's part is required.) It is truly awe-inspiring to wield a power so complete, and I am firm in my belief that the Aryan is the only race capable and truly qualified.

Baedecker and I have now mastered the commands enabling one to have control over a single zombie; however, as my colleague pointed out, we must learn how to control *groups* of them if we are to have any hope of marching a zombie army across Europe. Several other Bocors and Mambos in the encampment seem to have this ability, including Grandmarnier, who orders groups of zombies around with great ease and facility.

After some discussion, Baedecker and I are agreed that it is worth it to remain here a little longer to learn these somewhat more complicated "group commands." We shall then return to the Reich, carrying with us the momentous knowledge of how to create and command an army of zombies.

A final thought before I end this transmission: Our encounter with the late Father Gill was, of course, deeply troubling. The fact that an outsider could penetrate our cover is unnerving. (Perhaps Inspector Knecht's skills in deception are not as accomplished as he believes them to be.) After he was shot, we left Gill's body where it was, on the forest floor. A few hours later, it was not there, yet I have no doubt that the man was completely dead. He claimed to speak for Grandmarnier, but neither Grandmarnier nor anyone else in the village has remarked upon him (and we, certainly, have not brought it up in conversation). Could there have been truth to Gill's ravings that other European nations have previously attempted to learn and export zombie Voodoo technology? My own knowledge of Caribbean history suggests that it is possible. (Yet I am not surprised that representatives of the Third Reich are succeeding where those from lesser nations failed.) We must—in these final days in this country—insulate and protect ourselves from any others in Gill's cadre. It seems impossible that he operated alone, and we know not with whom he may have been aligned in his mission.

The incident with Gill illustrates that Baedecker and I are in mortal danger. However, we are also in the good graces of the most powerful Bocor in the country, armed with Lugers, and now in command of our own personal zombie named Hans.

I, for one, like our chances.

Yours respectfully,
Oswaldt Gehrin

COMMUNICATION 31

July 5, 1940
From: Oswaldt Gehrin
To: <u>Reinhard Heydrich</u>

My <u>Obergruppenführer</u>,

It is ironic that Inspector Knecht and the late Father Gill were ranged—in the priest's mind, at least—as opposites and enemies at cross-purposes, as *both* of them have now attempted to take our lives.

A few days ago, after making it clear to Grandmarnier that we needed to expand our zombie-commanding abilities to include large groups, the Bocor began a series of demonstrations intended to show us how the large-scale command we sought can be achieved. (Inspector Baedecker remains more trusted by Grandmarnier, and so it was my associate who worked most closely with the Voodoo elder.)

Early trials and demonstrations made it clear that Grandmarnier could control small groups of zombies (between five and ten) with ease and facility. The zombies were as obedient as if commanded one on one. As the number increased, however, there were noticeable breakdowns. With about fifteen zombies, one or two in the group would occasionally fail to respond to Grandmarnier's commands. He had to repeat himself two or three times to achieve the desired reaction. With thirty zombies—the most we had on hand for our trials—Grandmarnier demonstrated that he could reliably control about two-thirds of the group at a time. Obviously, this is an issue we shall have to address. (Whilst the idea of one German commander holding sway over an entire army of zombies is optimal—and may yet be achievable—Inspector Baedecker and I are also excited to imagine small zombie platoons each commanded by an individual Nazi Bocor.)

It is a different set of commands that is employed to command zombies in a group, and the intonation and delivery are substantially more difficult than the utterances used to direct a single subject. It is our desire to learn to deliver these commands with as much skill as Grandmarnier, and then to exceed him.

Less than an hour prior to this writing, a very striking thing happened.

As Baedecker and I were working on our group commands with a small squad of zombies (five of them, including Hans), we noticed a commotion at the edge of the encampment. Several of our neighboring Voodooists seemed to be disturbed by something just inside the tree line.

Suddenly the sound of gunfire rang out across the jungle. The nearby trees shook. The dirt at our feet danced. The

zombie next to me was hit by a round. (His chest puffed in a great explosion of dust, and he was momentarily unsteady on his feet.)

Then as suddenly as it had started, the firing ceased. Baedecker and I looked at one another. There could be no question that we (and perhaps our group of zombies) had been the intended targets. The encampment erupted into alarm. Several Voodooists took up firearms of their own—or machetes—and bounded into the jungle in all different directions.

"Look!" cried Baedecker.

I let my eyes follow his outstretched finger just in time to see Inspector Knecht lurking at the edge of the forest.

We produced our Lugers and fired back, but we failed to bring him down. Knecht beat a retreat as soon as we started firing. Within moments, he had disappeared entirely. A subsequent investigation of the spot where he had stood revealed only an empty clip from his MP 40. (At the time of this writing, many Voodooists are still searching the surrounding jungle for him.)

"Never fear," I said to Baedecker after it happened. "I shall explain this attack to Grandmarnier."

I stalked over to the old Bocor, who was accompanied by several attendants. Resplendent in an ornate headdress, his smile was absent and beatific like that of an enthusiast of Oriental meditation. For not the first time, his placid mien brought to my mind descriptions I have read of the Dalai Lama of Tibet and other spiritualists who are able to find transcendent placidity even in alarming situations.

"O Master Bocor," I said (for so we have fallen into the habit of calling Grandmarnier). "I have something important to tell you."

Grandmarnier looked at me with his bemused smile, as though I was a small child who claimed to have made a scientific discovery of bafflingly great importance.

"The man who just shot his gun into our encampment . . . he was trying to kill the two of us," I said, pointing over to Baedecker. "He is a former colleague of ours who has gone insane. He seeks to stop us from telling others of your wonderful teachings when we return to our homeland."

I stopped short, of course, of volunteering to depart for the safety of the Voodoo encampment.

"Oh," said Grandmarnier, as if what I had proposed was an absurdity. "But you can never leave us."

"Ahh," I said cautiously, forcing myself to return his strange smile.

Grandmarnier nodded at me placidly and idly strolled away, still in the company of his attendants.

Obviously, this attack by Inspector Knecht adds urgency and peril to our mission. It was a relief that Grandmarnier was not inclined to banish us from the village—on the contrary, our host seems to believe we intend to become permanent residents—but there remains the possibility of a subsequent attack. Baedecker and I have debated staging our own expedition to capture or kill Knecht, and have determined that the risks inherent in even a brief interruption to our work outweigh the benefits of eliminating the potential threat he poses. Thus, we are resolved that the best course of action is to redouble our efforts to master the manipulation and control of zombies. At the rate at which we are currently progressing, Baedecker believes it will only be a day or two before our acumen has progressed to a satisfactory level.

I long to return to the Fatherland—these weeks living amongst the Voodooists have given me an almost-indescribable longing for sauerbraten and beer. As I prepare to hand this encoded message to our runner (who shall pass it on to others, and then others still until it is finally left at the U-boat drop point), I do so with what I hope is the foreknowledge that this is the final missive I shall have to write, and that further updates can be provided to you in person.

After we have departed, I shall leave instructions with the Voodooists to kill our colleague in the most painful way they can devise. The traitorous nature of his attack on us may have endangered the entire Reich itself. For, my Obergruppenführer, I believe we are in possession of a power greater than any the world has known. Our undead soldiers shall prove a greater advancement to warfare than the development of bronze, the repeating rifle, or the Gatling gun!

Verily, we shall raise an army of these zombies and, so using them, crush the sum of the Fatherland's enemies until we rule the world forever!

Heil Hitler!
Oswaldt Gehrin

COMMUNICATION 32

July 5, 1940
From: Gunter Knecht
To: <u>Reinhard Heydrich</u>

<u>Obergruppenführer</u>,

Zombies are real.

Zombies are real. Zombies are real. Zombies are real.

I stare up at the Haitian moon that illuminates the page as I write these words . . . and can scarcely credit their truth. And yet I know it to be so. I have seen the evidence myself.

My suspicions have been wrong all this time. For, my dear, dear *Obergruppenführer*, zombies are real!

What happened was this: I was deep in the jungle. I had been traveling for hours and was exhausted. For days I had been searching for any clue as to the whereabouts of Baedecker and Gehrin. I had found nothing. I questioned every farmer and villager I encountered. I bribed those who seemed receptive to it and threatened those who were not. Yet every lead took me nowhere. I found myself directed to

white men who were not my colleagues, or else to
empty places where I found nothing.

I was distraught and tired. My canteen had been
empty for hours, and my feet ached terribly. I longed
to return to my temporary headquarters.

Cutting through a swath of forest as dusk began
to descend, I passed through a small village. I had
previously surveyed it and found nothing of value—
just a few straggling mud farmers and ramshackle
homes. However, I discovered that by night the place
changed remarkably. The settlement was a carnival
of Voodooists cavorting here, there, and every-
where! Some danced in strange circles. Some sat
together and spoke to one another quietly. Several
were preparing an evening's meal.

Then, in a lonely corner of the clearing, I saw them.

Gehrin and Baedecker. The former still wore the
uniform of a butterfly catcher, and the latter sported a
strange suit of feathers, drawings, and animal bones.
They stood beside a group of five or so Haitians,
who milled absently in front of them. Gehrin and
Baedecker were acting like drill sergeants, spitting
out commands in a strange guttural language. Some
of the group appeared to be reacting to these barked
orders, while others were less receptive.

Then a villager carrying a torch walked past the parading troops, and I saw that they were not Haitians at all . . . but *the reanimated bodies of the dead*!

There was no question about it. The ghastly figures had horrible, rotted skin that was falling from their bodies. Many lacked eyes, left with only empty soil-filled sockets. Worms crawled amidst what was left of their hair. They moved in a horrible shamble and often gnashed their teeth murderously. Indeed, their facial expressions seemed to indicate a ravenous madness that was barely being kept at bay.

I did not react rationally. I realize that now.

As an officer in the service of the Fatherland, I understand that I am expected to maintain my wits at all times. I must be unshakable. I know that. It is my responsibility. And yet the sight shook me utterly, to my core.

It was not only that these fools had been right all along about the existence of the walking dead. It was their arrogance. Their damned arrogance! The grins of confidence upon their idiot faces! These fools had stolen secrets that were rightfully the Reich's, and they clearly reveled in it. They looked so pleased with themselves. So full of hubris.

The fools . . .

No, my instincts told me, they were something worse than fools.

Traitors.

It could not stand.

Before I knew what was I was doing, my hand had flown to the MP 40 that hung from the strap over my shoulder. I loosed my bullets upon the impostors and their zombie parade.

In a matter of moments, my clip was expended. Baedecker, Gehrin, and their undead horde still stood. Everyone in the village looked around in alarm. Several villagers gestured in my direction. I instantly understood that I had acted rashly. (Soon these people would be after me.) Suddenly, as I was considering this, Baedecker and Gehrin produced their Lugers and fired back. I turned and fled into the jungle.

I ran until I thought my lungs would give out. The Voodooists pursued me relentlessly, yet I was always the quicker and the stealthier. I secreted myself within a mossy bog and waited motionless until the last of them gave up the chase.

Now, secure inside my new headquarters, I am plotting the destruction of Gehrin and Baedecker. They are untrustworthy outlaws. This is known for certain. They must be eliminated, and our mission, completed. I know where they are, and I know how to do it!

Prior experience—namely, Gehrin's evening spent singing with the Mambo—has already shown that a properly motivated Voodoo priest can divulge all the secrets necessary for the creation of zombies. Thus, I shall execute the traitors Gehrin and Baedecker and capture my own Voodoo priest. (If a fool like Gehrin can accomplish this task, then it should give me little trouble.) I shall then surrender myself (and my captive) to a U-boat crew. The interrogation can take place in Berlin. I know what to ask the Voodooist, and the secrets should come quickly once the interrogation gets underway. (Again, if Gehrin can do it . . .)

But first things first.

I acted rashly in the earlier encounter, allowing myself to be overcome by anger. Later this evening, I shall instead employ the cool precision for which we Germans are known. Armed to the very teeth, I shall return to the village of Voodooists, kill my traitorous cohorts, and then find a suitable hostage.

Thank you for being patient with me these many months, <u>Obergruppenführer</u>. I intend that—in just a few hours—your patience should be rewarded.

Respectfully,
Gunter Knecht

COMMUNICATION 33

July 6, 1940
From: Gunter Knecht
To: <u>Reinhard Heydrich</u>

Gehrin and Baedecker are dead. I have killed them.

I am sitting next to their bodies. Gehrin's face has been smashed beyond recognition, and his brains dashed out across the dirt floor. Baedecker has had an entire MP 40 clip emptied into his considerable chest.

For all their SD and RSHA training, it was surprisingly easy.

Just before dawn, I retraced my steps and found the Voodoo village. It was wrapped in a strange, thick fog that gave the place a ghostly aspect. Many torches and cooking fires still burned, but it appeared that the residents had retired for the night (or departed from the village entirely). Neither man nor zombie moved. All was stillness. All was silence.

Concealing myself in the shadows, I crept to the place where I had seen Gehrin and Baedecker directing their zombie parade. Directly adjacent was a modest hut with a thatched roof. I moved in close and looked through the open doorway of the hovel. Inside, Gehrin and Baedecker slept peacefully on straw mattresses. I crept inside stealthily, intending to do the both of them in with my knife.

Suddenly, Gehrin's eyes opened. He saw me, sat bolt upright, and exclaimed, "You!"

Instinct took over. I dropped my knife and readied my gun. Gehrin was quick, though, and pounced on me like a jungle cat. With an acrobatic move remembered from my combat training, I caught his blow and used his own momentum to send him careening to the ground. Then, before Baedecker could rise, I turned my MP 40 upon him and pulled the trigger. (I intended to shoot him only twice, but in the fury of the moment, I emptied the entire clip into his massive body!) I then turned back to Gehrin, who was only just righting himself. Gripping his head, I brought his face down on a wooden stool. It seemed to knock him unconscious. Taking no chances, I gripped the stool like a club and beat it against his head—again and again—until his brains were literally dashed out.

I then reloaded my submachine gun and prepared for the onrush of Voodooists certain to come. (My weapon's blasting had been loud. Even a single shot

should have been enough to awaken the village's lighter sleepers.) I paused at the doorway to the hut, looking out into the dark village and flickering torches beyond.

But nothing stirred.

Was an attack building? Were the Voodooists coordinating a movement against me?

I waited, my MP 40 at the ready. Then I waited some more. Then more still.

Nothing.

Still hesitant, I knelt down in the hut next to the corpses of the traitors and considered my next move. Dawn broke slowly, but the fog stayed where

it was. Though the sun was now upon the horizon, this ethereal mist—which was quite thick and dense—still made the village a strange and dreamlike place.

Confident that if attacked I could simply disappear into the clouds all around me, I summoned the resolve to leave the hut. I still intended to kidnap a Bocor or Mambo as quickly as possible and then to make my way to a U-boat.

Yet something very strange had occurred.

The village—which I had seen populated by twenty or thirty people by day, and which was a veritable social gathering at night—was totally deserted. I moved from hovel to hovel and found every home empty. Stalking through the thick fog, I encountered neither man nor beast. Within thirty minutes' time, I had made a thorough search of the entire place and found not one person. Signs of recent habitation were all around, but there were no people. It gave me the uneasy feeling of having accidentally wandered onto an empty theater stage just before a performance.

Though impossible, I began to feel as though I had dreamed the village as it had been—populated and lively.

I crept back through the smothering fog to the hut of Baedecker and Gehrin. I half-expected them to have disappeared too, but they were just as I had left them.

I am sitting now in the hut, preparing this message for you. The fog has abated slightly as the sun has moved higher in the sky, but the village remains deserted. I have resolved to take a quick nap here on the hut's floor—I am very exhausted from the night's work—and then to press on.

This was not a totally optimal outcome, and I admit that freely. However, the elimination of Gehrin and Baedecker is an important accomplishment (for which, I can only trust, I will find myself congratulated at a later date). I shall make it my mission in the coming hours and days to capture a Bocor or a Mambo capable of singing the zombie-creating song, and then return swiftly to Berlin.

I now know *exactly* what I must do. The power of the zombie will soon be within the grasp of the Reich!

I am, my dear <u>Obergruppenführer</u>, so very, very close.

Respectfully,
Gunter Knecht

COMMUNICATION 34

July 5, 1940
From: Oswaldt Gehrin
To: Reinhard Heydrich

My Obergruppenführer,

A disaster has occurred. Our mission shall yet be salvaged, but I hasten to report a crippling catastrophe.

No sooner did I hand off my previous encrypted letter to our Haitian courier than I found Inspector Baedecker reclining motionless inside our dwelling, looking distraught and unwell. He was slumped in the corner, and the color seemed to have drained from his face. His hand clutched his side, and I saw blood pooling beneath him.

"Baedecker, what has happened?" I cried.

He responded that one of Knecht's bullets had entered his side during the attack.

"What?" I cried. "But I saw none of his bullets strike you! And you said nothing at the time!"

Baedecker revealed that he first believed it to have been a mere grazing, not sanguinary or worthy of mention. But the folds of his stomach are many . . . On first inspection, he had missed the spot where the bullet had punctured his

U.S. Army Signal Intelligence Service
WASHINGTON 25, D.C.

UNCLASSIFIED

The transmissions in this dossier have thus far been presented in the order in which they were intercepted by the U.S. Signals Intelligence Service (as outgoing transmissions from German U-boats).

The above letter is an exception. It was never transmitted (and we believe its contents still remain unknown to the RSHA). Rather, it was recovered from the body of a German RSHA agent believed to be Gunter Knecht on July 6, 1940. The body was found in an abandoned village deep in the Haitian jungle east of Port-au-Prince by a squad of five U.S. Marines. (This marine incursion was classified Top Secret and was unknown to the Haitian government, but it was authorized by the Department of War and the Signals Intelligence Service pursuant to the information contained in previous transmissions.)

The marines arrived at the village in question on the same day Knecht is believed to have penned the above letter, which he had not yet encrypted. (In their report, the marines also noted an unusually thick fog that seemed to surround the village.)

Knecht's body was found in a prone position inside a small hut. The back of his head had been opened and its contents were missing. The surrounding skull and flesh bore human teeth marks, giving the commanding marine the impression that "his brains had been eaten."

On the floor adjacent to Knecht was a body believed to be that of RSHA operative Oswaldt Gehrin. His head appeared to have been crushed with a nearby wooden stool, consistent with the manner described in the letter written by Operative Knecht. There was no sign of RSHA operative Franz Baedecker.

Upon the body of Operative Gehrin, the following letter was found. (Please note that it was written prior to the final message of Operative Knecht.) It was also unsent, and is the final piece of correspondence contained in this report.

side. Now it was clear that he was dying from a slug that had traveled deep within him.

"Surely you can be saved," I said (though the corpselike sheen already creeping over his face seemed to indicate otherwise).

Baedecker said that he was lost.

"Can I do anything to ease your suffering at least?" I asked my colleague. "We have morphine packets somewhere, I think."

Baedecker replied that only one thing would bring him solace: I must agree to reanimate his body, and *make him the very first Nazi zombie of the Third Reich*!

Tearfully, I nodded and said I would make it so.

Baedecker smiled and lay back against the side of the hut. Moments later, he passed away.

In the ensuing moments, I found a Bocor from the village who was versed in the second voice of the Song of the Jeje. Together, we sang Baedecker back to life.

The zombified Baedecker is under my control completely. I can see the familiar murderous look in his eyes (which denotes every zombie's true inclination), but I have mastered

the magic words enough to keep him placid and harmless as a lamb. As I write this, I have ordered him to recline next to me in our hut. He obeys without question. It is remarkable. (It is one thing to see members of an inferior race respond obediently to commands issued by an Aryan, but quite another to see one of my fellow Germans rendered so completely under my control.)

In light of these developments, my <u>Obergruppenführer</u>, I am terminating our operations here.

In the morning, I shall return to one of our U-boat posts directly and wait to be discovered. (I may well arrive before this letter does.) I am confident that I can now reproduce both voices in the Song of the Jeje myself. I am also confident that any further refining of the controls necessary to control large groups of zombies is something that can be done in Berlin.

I shall bring the zombified Baedecker with me. He is "living" proof that the Reich can now coax its own dead to rise from the fields of battle to fight once again for the Fatherland. He will likewise demonstrate that the murderous instincts of the zombie—however powerful—can be completely restrained by a qualified Voodoo master. (The U-boat crew on our journey back to Germany will be in no danger of having their brains eaten by him . . . unless I am somehow incapacitated or killed. And even then, I'm told it takes nearly an hour for a Bocor's final command upon a zombie to "wear off.")

Yours respectfully,
Oswaldt Gehrin

Postscript: Strange . . . I stepped outside our house to find our runner just now, and the village seems entirely deserted. An unexpected, ghostly mist is descending. It is difficult to walk more than a few feet without becoming disoriented. I shall wait until dawn to deliver this letter, and perhaps sleep some more in the meantime.